Previous

Boss

The next day

"What up my G. What's good?" I said dapping up my nigga who'd walked up to me outside the trap house. I had met up with my lawyers this morning and was feeling good about the money I had come up on from staying in that bitch for three years for wrongful imprisonment. Truthfully, I was guilty as a muthafucka, but I would still take that twenty grand a year to flip into a larger amount.

"Yo, Ahmad see who that is!" Steez yelled to our newest general who was down the street, next to the stop sign.

I saw it was a silver Jaguar and I knew that was Lump ass coming to fuck with me.

"That car cool. They for me," I was letting things slowly fizzle out with Lump after getting back with Megan. Dropping bitches too fast often made them crazy so I was letting her down easy.

I got inside her passenger seat, and she turned down the Keysha Cole playing through her speaker.

"Yo, what's up Ma? You good?" I said to Lump who was sitting in the front seat in a T-shirt, sweats, and a ponytail.

"Yeah baby, I'm good. Just been tired. Couldn't sleep. Wanted to see you," she said reaching over to my face.

"You good though?" I asked as Lump sat there in silence biting her bottom lip.

"What's wrong with you?"

"Hmm?"

"I said what's wrong with you? Why are you looking like that?" I repeated myself turning toward Lump who had a strange look on her face.

"It's nothing Boss. I mean it's something but it's not bad."

"Well, what is it about? Me not coming to stay with you lately?"

"No! It's not that."

"Then what is it?"

"I'm scared to tell you."

"Lump stop playing muh fuckin games with me and tell me what's up." I turned towards her body.

"I'm pregnant," she said looking over to me who was stuck with one facial expression. I exhaled deeply and then looked out the window hoping to find the right words to say to not drive this hoe up the wall.

"Okay, so what are you going to do?"

"What you mean Boss?"

"What you gone do about the baby? You getting rid of it right?"

"I'm not getting an abortion."

"Why not? Me and you are not together. We never have been." I had to keep it real with her. This wasn't a time to tiptoe around the hoe feelings.

"Boss, I don't need you to have that attitude right now. I need you to be supportive and not just thinking about killing our baby."

"And I need you to be supportive too! You know I got a lot of shit going on. I can't be thinking about no shit like that right now. Niggas trying to kill me, and you want me to bring another child into this world. Hell nah," I replied adjusting myself in the seat.

"Boss you need to take a step back okay, I don't need you to watch me or feed me or even take care of me," she replied getting an attitude.

"Then what is it? What do you need from me?"

"For you to be a father to our child," she said grabbing her stomach. Lump started to cry seeing the expression on my face but even her tears didn't move me. The only tears I cared about were my mama's, my girl's, and my daughter's. That's it.

"Serenity I'm not about to shut you out but you don't get that this shit bigger than us."

"What's bigger than it though? Who, Megan? The bitch who you been staying with? My cousin already showed me the girl's page. Don't forget Chicago isn't that big, Boss." she said bringing up the very shit I didn't need her knowing about. Was this why she was all of a sudden pregnant and trying to lock me down?

"Meg don't have nothing to do with this."

"You're right. With or without her in the picture, we still have a baby on the way. And I want to keep it. I want to raise it with you."

"Do you fuck with me Serenity?"

"Yes, you know I do."

"And do you love me?"

"Yes, unfortunately," she replied wiping a tear from her face with the back of her hand.

"Well if you love me then just think about this and remember everything, I got going on right now. I fuck with you tough and I wanna be with you one day, I just wanna get myself all the way together first," I said trying to convince Lump I was keeping it real with her instead of bullshitting her like I was.

She sat there quietly wrapping her arms around her stomach as she put her head on the steering wheel.

"It's alright baby, I promise you. You know daddy got you," I said leaning over in the seat to pull her closer to me.

"Here, stop crying. Wipe your face, you alright," I said taking my thumb under her eye.

"Head to the house, take a shower, and I'll be there later to tuck you in and talk tonight."

"Okay." She still seemed upset.

"No. Look at me. I have love for you Serenity. I want to be with you and make plenty of babies in the future but not right now. Just let me get rid of my baggage and I will be all yours. You going to listen to me, right baby?" I asked grabbing her chin, getting that little smirk she always gave me.

"Okay, I understand. I'll get rid of it but only for the betterment of our future." She said the exact words I was looking for.

"Good, I appreciate that baby, for real."

"Well, I guess I will head home, and I'll see you there," she said backing away from my arms.

"I'll stop by and get some chicken to cook too. I know you're hungry."

"Hell yeah," I replied, before kissing her on the lips. I slipped my tongue in her mouth and held her body close enough to make her think I meant it.

If this was what I had to do to keep Lump happy to get rid of the baby, then I would string her on for a little longer. And if she didn't get rid of it soon, I would have to get rid of her because ain't shit fucking up what me and Megan got going on.

Megan

Today had been a pretty chill day besides the fact I had been dealing with Kit's psychotic ass texts all day while servicing clients. This girl had sent me over 40 messages, been on Facebook, and in my inbox. I was twenty seconds away from filing a police report if she didn't leave me the fuck alone.

"Is that bitch calling you again?" Yana asked, standing next to me hearing my phone go off yet again.

"Yes, it's her. This bitch just won't get the fuckin' drift," I replied rolling my eyes and forwarding the call again.

"I don't know why you won't just let Boss kill her, that would make it a lot easier on y'all," she replied thinking it would be that simple to solve all my problems with murder. It sounded good but I couldn't let that shit go down for several reasons, one being Boss didn't need to get in any more trouble.

If Kit magically popped up dead and people saw I was back with Boss, they would put two and two together quickly. I felt it was best to let Kit possibly kill herself. The way she was texting me, I could see that coming soon.

After I was done with my 11:00 appointment, I took the time to sweep up the floor and then took a seat with a bag of my favorite chips. My feet hurt but I had one more client before going home. We had the television playing the new Tyler Perry Movie, and I was going to enjoy that until my next appointment arrived.

I was so into the movie that when the door chime rang, I didn't realize who it was until he started talking.

"Yo, yo, what's up? Y'all bitches get up and do something. Y'all don't have no clients," Boss said walking into the shop demanding attention at the door. He was wearing a nice pair of jeans and an Amiri shirt with his newest Cuban link chain. Even with his beard being a little scraggly, he still looked fresh and oh-so-clean. My pussy was instantly ready looking at this man. Sometimes I think Boss is even too fine for me.

"Hey baby, I was just about to call you when this movie went off," I said looking up from my chair as Boss leaned over to give me a kiss.

"Hey, Brother," Yana spoke.

"What up Yana?" Boss replied making me get up to sit in his lap.

"Why you over here? What's going on babe?"

"Nothing just stopped by to see what you were doing. Seeing if you will be home early today?"

"Probably not, I had a huge gap in between appointments and my next one is boho braids. I will probably be making it home around 7:00."

"That's alright, I'll probably be at the trap all night anyway. We have a large shipment coming in. I have to make sure everything gets distributed right since Mystic is still not on his feet yet," he said sounding like the overprotective control freak he always was with his money. Boss never really trusted anyone but me, Mys, and Steez so I knew he couldn't wait for him to get out of the hospital.

"Hey, Yana, you think you can line me up real quick?"

"Twenty-dollar squeeze in fee. You paying?" she replied sticking her hand out.

"Bitch don't do my man like that. You know if I could do it I would."

"Well, learn how to do it so he can stay out of my chair. Come on Boss man, let me hook you up," Yana directed Boss and he went over to her chair.

When he sat down, she put the cape over him, and I took this opportunity to stop the calls constantly coming to my phone.

"I'll be right back, I gotta call the light company before 6:00," I said hopping up out of the chair and running to the back to answer Kit and cuss her ass out. I'd done it a few times before, but I was hoping each time she got a better view of the bigger picture. We were done.

"What is it, Kit? What do you want? Why do you keep calling me?"

"What I want is for you to answer me. It's been three weeks and all I can get is bullshit-ass responses and a porno from you and that nigga! You can't possibly think it's okay to play the game like that?" Kit sounded as if she wanted to cry.

"Kit, I have tried cutting you off a million different ways, but you won't listen."

"Why should I? Megan, I love you!"

"But I don't want this anymore Kit! Please listen. You're acting like a fuckin stalker and that ain't you!" I raised my voice but not high enough for Yana and Boss to hear,

"How could you switch up on me like that? One minute you're gay then all of a sudden you like dick again? You are all over the fucking place! You don't know what the fuck you want and it's sad!"

"Kit I was never gay, I just vibed with you and thought you were a good person. I am bisexual. And Boss's dick ain't have nothing to do with this. You showed me you were no different than him! The only reason he hasn't killed you yet is because of me. Show him some respect and leave Chicago. One day he not gone give a fuck what I think." I reminded Kit who was playing with her life even contacting me.

"So, did you ever love me, Meg?"

"Yes."

"Did you ever respect me?"

"Yes, Kit!"

"So why did you just cut me off like that? You blocked my old number and changed the locks on the crib. You just said fuck the operation we had going on and everything. Why would you give up on making your own money? You know we had the coke game on lock Megan. You just going to give that up?" Kit asked, bringing up the fact we had once been partners in our own little drug ring. It was cool being over money and learning the ins and outs of the game, but I had no problems leaving all that to Boss. Fuck what I said before.

"Look Kit the money was cool, and I appreciate everything we made but I don't wanna be involved with drugs anymore. Now my shop is clear of all illegal activity and I wanna keep it that way. I don't have to worry about losing my license or the whole shop in general to the cops," I said to Kit who immediately got quiet not hearing what she wanted to hear.

"But look I gotta get back to my clients. I'm sorry shit had to happen this way, but it just did. I hope you find yourself Kit and I hope you find happiness one day. Please just let me be. I have to go now," I said only hearing a dial tone afterwards. Hopefully, I had pressed the right buttons, and she would leave me alone for good.

Knock. Knock. Knock.

"Aye Baby, I'm about to run out now. Hurry up so I can rub on your booty," Boss said as I flew out the door to my man. I wasn't about to let Kit ruin my day or waste my time.

"I'll see you soon Daddy."

"Love you big booty," he said grabbing a handful of my ass and laying those big juicy lips onto mine.

"Y'all are just too cute." Yana admired us from the side. I know she was probably having an I told you so moment with me. She knew I couldn't let this man go before I did.

Once Boss was gone, I chilled a little longer until my client came in

"Hey sis, just a wash and the braids, right?"

"Yes, and I need dye treatment too. I am getting grey hair because of that son of mine. He's letting Chicago consume him."

"I sure hate to hear that. When I first started doing your hair, he was sweet."

"Girl times have changed for sure. Now we have to be cautious of our own kids in our house." We both shook our heads because it was the truth.

Bing

When the doorbell rang, I saw it was Miss Debra. Yana customer slash sister wife.

"Hello, how's everyone doing?"

"Hey." Me and my client spoke. As Yana walked from around her chair.

"Miss Debra. I didn't have you down for today. Did I make a mistake girlfriend?" Yana asked, but Debra suddenly pulled out a gun.

"Hoe, you've been fucking my husband! I thought you were my friend!" She proclaimed, just before she pulled the trigger twice sending Yana back on the floor. I screamed to the top of my lungs and Miss Debra ran out of the door as I fell to the floor next to my friend.

"Call 911!"

Kit

"I'm sorry shit had to happen this way, but it just did. I hope you find yourself Kit and I hope you find happiness one day. Please just let me be. I have to go now."

When the recording stopped, I took no time asking the questions I had.

"So, was that good enough? Was that all you needed her to say?" I asked the detectives after they listened to the recording of me and Meg's earlier conversation.

I'd made up my mind hours ago I wasn't going to just let Megan play me like a fool. She had some nerve trying to act as if she was doing me a favor by getting Boss to 'spare my life'. I was on a mission to get her to reap what she sows, and cry plenty of nights behind bars just likeBoss.

"So, now that we have the recording, we just want to make sure we have everything lined up to take to the D.A., Megan Fox was over running drug money through the shops that you two own?"

"Yes sir."

"And she was well aware that the money came from illegal activities?"

"Yes sir."

"And we're going to find evidence of this in bank deposits, financial records?"

"Yes, it should all be there."

"You are aware that you will have to testify in court?" he said making my stomach hurt thinking about being on the stand.

"I'm well aware of that and the consequences that come with it for me turning myself in. I'm ready to deal with what comes with it so I can move on with my life. I want out!" I said taping my fist against the table making a thudding noise in the silent room.

"Well, okay Ms. Harrington. We're going to verify all this information before taking it to the D.A. Don't leave out of Chicago."

"Oh, I'm not."

"Take care of yourself. See you soon," he said sticking his hand out like we were patnas.

No lie, I hated shaking the pig's hand but if it helped me get the best revenge on the ones, I hated then I would do so. I wonder how long Boss would hold Megan down once she got locked up. Probably about as long as she did. He will probably have a new bitch by the time Megan is booked in.

When I got back to the hotel I unlocked my room door, juggling Harold's Chicken in one hand. I know I was supposed to be keeping a low profile with all Boss's goons looking for me, but this chicken and mild sauce was calling my name. I figured I might as well eat good before getting locked up for I don't know how many years.

"Damn it's cold in here," I said to myself putting the chicken on the desk as I walked over to the air unit in the window. I cut that bitch down to low cool and kicked off my shoes to take off my socks and get in the shower.

I unbuckled my pants remembering to take my wallet out just before dropping them to the floor. I headed to the restroom, cut on the shower, and began to take off my sports bra as I heard a loud thud outside the front door.

"Fuck is that?" I said cutting off the water and grabbing a towel to wrap around my waist. I dashed out the restroom door and ran across the double beds trying to get to my gun on the nightstand. Even though I was moving fast, I still didn't make it there in time before four men in black ski masks rushed into my hotel room.

"Get on the floor! Right now! This ain't a game!"

"What you looking over there for, huh? Get your ass on the ground?" one of them said noticing I was eyeing my gun on the counter. My towel dropped to the floor, and I had on nothing but a sports bra.

"Hwissssss!" One of them whistled out of the door and then shut it shortly after.

"Look man, if y'all gone kill me just do it now! I don't have shit to lose anyway," I said right before Boss walked through the door,

"Well, well, well, it is true. You do have a pussy underneath them clothes," he said walking into the room and taking off his jacket.

"Whatever pussy nigga I'm not scared of you! Do what you gotta do to me! I don't have shit to live for! Fuck you bitch!" I screamed spitting on Boss's shoes.

"Damn baby, you might want to save some of that saliva in case you need it to try and save your life. It's a lot of dicks in here to suck and none of us nut easy," he said sending flames up my spine.

"What the fuck does that mean? How about you suck my dick pussy,"

They all started to laugh.

"Oh, I brought somebody else to see you. Do you remember this nigga? Ahmad, take off your mask bruh," Boss said directing the smallest nigga to reveal he was the one I had hired to kill him a while ago.

"You see Kit or Kitina I should say. Everybody in here are real niggas but you. Nobody wants to see real niggas off the streets but rat niggas like yourself."

"Fuck you! I should've walked up and killed your ass a long time ago! You dirty as they come. You and that hoe deserve each other.

"Yeah, you're right, we do deserve each other. She's a bad bitch and I'm a boss ass nigga. But what are you? A pretender with nice tits and some baggy clothes?" he said kneeling beside me.

"Don't you dare touch me nigga. Just put a bullet in my head! I ain't with that gay shit."

"Don't worry lil mama. I don't want your pussy. I'm well taken care of; shit I can go to her shop right now and get some pussy in the backroom. It was always fun to us doing it with other people in the room. Just like that night, we fucked in the restroom when I robbed your dumb ass," he said slapping me on the side of my thigh.

"So, that was you! I knew you had to be the one to convince my boy to turn on me!"

"Who, your boy? Ahmad?"

"No Dezzy! Your flaw ass knew he was the realest nigga I had around me and probably made a bunch of broken promises to him." I replied as Boss started laughing and rubbing his gun against his temple.

"Oh, so you thought your patna was in on the robbery?"

"Hell yeah, I do. I know."

"Nah, you wrong about this Young M.A. Unlike you, I only fuck with niggas who are loyal to me. Somebody that established in your crew can't do nothing for me," he said being the arrogant narcissist he was.

"Stop lying Boss! I know Dezzy helped you that night."

"He really didn't. Actually, it's a family reunion here tonight. These the same niggas I robbed you with." You are dumb as fuck. I can't wait to kill you," he said, and I charged towards him because I was tired of hearing his shit. Before I could even get off the floor, I was pistol-whipped by the nigga closest to me. As I laid there with my head against the carpet, I caught a glimpse of the nigga that hit me shoes and grew a lump in my throat. They were just like the ones I accused Dezzy of wearing. What the fuck did I do?

"Calm down Killa. Sit up, and catch your breath. You are alright," Boss said throwing me against the wall.

"Why are you so mad shorty? What is it, Megan never told you it was us that robbed you?"

I didn't respond.

"Damn, I guess she really didn't fuck with you," he said as I leaned against the wall, blood and tears running down my face. I sat there in silence as he continued talking, thinking about all the shit I'd done to get to this point.

Number one thing was not taking out Boss when he killed Tony and dragging this shit on for so long. Number two was falling in love with a bitch that couldn't see past what was right and just wanting to be that bitch. I had given Megan my all but at the end of the day that didn't matter. She's shown me her true fucked up colors.

"Steez past me the silencer," he said and then the nigga with the beard tossed him the metal piece. Boss took out his gun and started putting the silencer on the barrel.

"Any last words lil mama?" he asked as my nerves shot through the roof looking at the barrel of his gun. I couldn't believe this shit, I couldn't believe I was about to die like this. Nah, man, I change my mind. I'm not ready to die.

"Listen, Boss, I know you don't wanna hear it but killing me won't solve anything, I can help you if you spare my life, I will work for you! I'll hook you up with my plug so you can have shipments coming in from everywhere. I can even tell the cops I was lying about Megan. I was just talking shit. I'm not ready to die." I pleaded, but Boss still pointed the gun down to my head.

Boss

Ppsssuu, Ppsssuu, Ppsssuu

Rang out from the pistol and Kit's body dropped down to the ground.

"Steez, you got that spray paint on you, right?"

"Yeah, I got it."

"Iight, spray MS-13 shit all over this muthafucka. Ahmad, y'all go start the car," I said directing my niggas as I wiped Kit's blood from over my face.

"Look at you, died on your knees where you should have been your whole life. Didn't they tell you not to fuck with me? I'm untouchable." I kicked her body over.

When I left the hotel where Kit was, we went back to Mys trap where I'd left my phone. I grabbed it from the charger in the corner and saw Megan had called me over fifty times and rang in again before I could dial out.

"Megan, what's wrong?"

"It's Yana Boss! Miss Debra shot her."

"Who? Who shot who?"

"One of Yana's clients came in and shot her. I'm up at the hospital now but it doesn't look too good. She lost a lot of blood. They are trying but they said to prepare for the worst."

"Damn, what hospital yall at baby?"

"University."

"I'm on my way." I hung up the phone and sped off towards the hospital. After driving like a maniac for twenty minutes I parked my car outside the front doors and hopped out.

"Sir, you can't park there."

"Tow the mutha fucka, I don't give a fuck." I rushed into the emergency room. In the waiting area, I spotted Megan sitting near the window still crying her eyes out.

I kneeled in front of her and hugged around her waist while she cried like a baby.

"You been up here by yourself baby?"

"No, Mrs. Tracy is here too." She was barely able to get out in between sniffles.

"She's a wreck but she just took Adayah to the restroom."

She replied, just as I heard Adayah's voice in the near distance. When I turned around, I caught eyes with Adayah and that's when I realized, I never should've come up here. My baby didn't know that she was supposed to be a secret.

"Daddy!" Adayah ran over to me and jumped into my arms.

Mrs. Tracey knew the truth, but Megan was now looking at us with a puzzled expression on her face.

"Wait, did she just call you daddy?"

Claimed By The Hood Millionaire: 2

Chapter 1

Boss

The look on Megan's face made me scared to speak. I haven't been scared much in my life, but this was a time I was afraid.

"Daddy! Can I get a toy? Please please please!"

Adayah asked, unaware of what was happening right now. Her daddy felt like he was about to lose his life and most importantly the woman he loves.

Megan kneeled next to us and held Adayah's hand.

"TT baby, this is not your dad. This is Boss, he's my boyfriend." She spoke and Tracy and I met eyes.

"I know that his name is Boss but he's my daddy." Adayah hugged my neck, and I couldn't do anything but drop my head.

"Honey, you're just confused. This is not your dad and Boss, why are you not saying anything? Tell her you are not her daddy." Megan's voice cracked since my silence was getting the best of her.

"Baby, can we go outside and talk about this away from her?" Megan started shaking her head and backing away.

"What do we have to talk about Boss? Tell this poor baby that she is not your kid. Why can't you just say that? She's going through enough as it is!"

"Megan she is my kid. She's saying that because she knows me, and she knows that I am her dad. I saw her a lot when I was locked up but it's a really long story so can we please step outside?" I finally made eye contact with her which crushed a nigga heart. She looked like something was stuck in her throat and she couldn't swallow it, so the pain was just sitting there. And her eyes looked sunken in just that quickly with no soul behind them, it's like my confession had sucked the life out of her.

"You mean to tell me that you two mutha fuckas." She pressed her lips together tightly and shut her eyes, so I knew she was mad.

"Boss, let's go outside, now!" She walked away, and I gave Adayah to Tracey.

Megan was walking full speed to the parking lot and in between the cars as I chased her down. When she finally stopped, she turned around and slapped me so hard my spit hit the car window next to us.

"My best friend you dirty dog!" She kept swinging and punching me as I tried to dodge her licks.

"Megan chill! It was not what you think. It never happened without you there. I've never fucked Yana by myself. We both cared about your ass too much for that!"

"How the fuck am I supposed to believe that? How long have you known about that little girl?" She stopped hitting me to point toward the lobby.

"Pretty much her whole life."

"Wow, and y'all were going to keep it from me because I didn't deserve the truth? Huh? Is that what it is? Tell me!" Her chocolate skin almost had a red tent to it just as her eyes did.

"Megan, you abandoned me in prison shortly after I found out about her. At that point, there was no point in telling you. The last time you came to see me and thought a random girl was there, it was Yana the whole time. We were discussing how to tell you about Adayah." She grabbed her hair and walked in circles with her hands over her head.

"That dirty bitch."

"Megan, I asked for her to come after we found out she was mine. I wanted to meet her." Megan started stroking her hair back away from her face.

"How is she your kid when you can't even have kids."

"She's mine, Megan."

"She can't be. Before you went to jail, we tried to have a baby for a year and nothing happened, so how the fuck did you just pop up with a kid?"

The conversation went silent, and I dropped my head seeing the realization set into her face.

"Oh, wow." She started to shake her head slowly.

"It really must be me then. I'm the broken one. The dumb one. The one that handed her best friend her man."

She started to walk off. I grabbed her arms from behind and she wrestled to break away from me.

"Megan stop. You didn't give me away to anyone. Just because Adayah is my kid doesn't mean I want Yana or a family with her. I never would've even touched the girl had y'all not approached me about fucking around. Liquor and you are the reason Adayah is here, and you need to admit that. It's not just because I snaked you with your best friend."

Megan let out a loud ass scream before dropping down to the ground. I tried to bend down and console her, but she stepped back away from me.

"Leave me alone Boss. Just please, leave me alone." She kept backing away from me. She continued to walk backward until car lights shined across her body. I hurried and pulled her back towards me, and she was barely missed by the car passing by.

"You alright baby?"

"I'm fine! I'm good. Get off of me." She pulled her arms away from me. This time when she walked off, I let her because I knew she needed time to cool off. I knew where to find her, so it was probably best to just let her be tonight.

On my way back into the hospital my phone started to ring from my pockets, and I reached for it quickly thinking it was Megan. It however was Steez who was taking Kit's body to be disposed of.

"Yo, what's up?" I asked, walking to the lobby.

"Bro we can't find this bitch anywhere!"

"Can't find who, what the fuck you talking about nigga?"

"The dike bitch Kit. We put her ass in the trunk, and she must've gotten out when we went inside the trap to get some smoke."

"But how? I shot her ass at least four times."

"Shit, I know nigga, I was there. We looking for her now but she may have already bled out somewhere while hiding out."

"Man fuck! Yall niggas know I don't like when my bodies are found somewhere. We need to get her ass back ASAP!" I yelled in the middle of the parking lot. Tonight was feeling like the end of the world and if Kit made it to the cops, it in fact was.

Chapter 2

Megan

Anytime I was going through anything I wanted to talk to my mama. She wasn't the most religious mother out there, but she had wisdom beyond my years. There was always something about the way she worded things that made everything make sense to me. Without her, I never would have gotten over Boss the first time.

Knock, knock, knock, knock

"Mama, open up, it's me, Megan."

I banged on the doorway too long for my liking. This was my childhood home, and I knew you could hear this loud wooden door from any part of this house. Her car being outside and her not answering the door sent my pressure through the roof. I hated that she lived here alone but I also knew she was never moving from her house.

Since my adolescent days, I knew that you could easily access the house through my old bedroom window. I'd tweaked it a long time ago to where the window never locked even when the lever was down. Now I was wondering had my old trick exposed my mama to something dangerous lurking around. Especially my psycho ex-girlfriend who had lost her mind.

With those fears in my head, I decided to go inside to see if my mother was okay. I jumped the side fence and the family's yard dog Lucky came barking inches away from my ankles.

Roof! Ahroof roof

"Quiet boy, hush. You remember me." I walked along the side of the house unsure if he actually did. Once I reached my window, I slid it open, and I heard my mama screaming at the top of her lungs.

"Lord! Help me! Jesus!"

"Oh my God! I'm coming, mama!" I cried out, climbing through that window as fast as I could. I ran down the hall and into her room where her screams seemed to be coming from. When I swung the door open, nothing could prepare me for what I saw in front of me.

"Daddy?"

I stared in shock at my fifty-five-year-old mother straddled over my estranged father. I shut the door and placed my hand on my forehead as I walked into the living room.

After sitting on the couch to catch my breath, my mama soon rushed out of the room to plead her case to me. She knew he was the last man on earth I wanted to see. Especially here with her.

"Baby girl, I can explain."

"Really, him mama. You let him back here?"

"Megan he's changed I promise you. He was in rehab, and he's been clean for some time now." She was unable to make eye contact as she spoke. She knew her being with my father was the lowest thing she could do. She knew exactly what he did to me.

"Clean from drugs but still very much dirty on the inside."

"No, he's not. Drugs were his downfall, and you know that. He was a good father to you."

"A good father?" I stood up, yelling at this point.

"That man molested me, mama. I was just a child! He ruined me and took my innocence away! How could you forget that!"

"Baby, I told you that was just a bad dream that you had back in the day. It did not happen."

"No, it wasn't, and you fucking know that! I can't believe you right now mama!" I stood up, so irate I could be heard across the house. To think I came over here on a warpath because of Boss and Yana only to be sent completely over the edge by my mama's betrayal.

"What is the problem in here?" That nigga walked out of the back room in his boxers, and I turned my head.

"Mama, I told you I didn't want to see him ever again! I hate this man because of what he did to me, and he's caused you nothing but stress and pain! Why are you putting yourself through this again?"

"You weren't supposed to see him today, Megan. How did you even get in here."

"Through the window! So, are you letting him come back now?"

"He's changed, Megan!"

"Really mommy, really!" The broken-hearted child that I'd buried deep inside was now seeping through the cracks of my eyes as tears.

"Megan, your daddy and I are trying to figure things out as we go."

"If that's the case then I'm gone and you're dead to me."

"Don't say that."

"I mean it, so make a choice!"

I walked to the door and my sperm donor grabbed my arm. Something about him touching me made me go crazy and I started windmill punching him harder than I'd hit Boss at the hospital.

"Megan, stop!" My mama fussed, attempting to pull me away from him. I didn't stop punching on him until I was physically tired.

"Don't touch me! Don't fucking touch me."

"Foxy girl you are tripping. Why are you doing me this way? Daddy never hurt you. I wouldn't do that. I'm not a sick man that would."

"Yes, you did, and I don't care what you say! You hurt me bad that summer you and Mama separated! You kept me at your house for a month so no one would know how you ruined me! You're probably the reason why I can't have kids now! And I hate you!" My voice cracked as I'm sure veins protruded from my neck.

"Meg baby, why don't you take a seat and speak with your father and me? You know I love you and your dad loves you too. As far as his addiction, he's gotten help."

"Bye, mama. You can stay here and fuck with this pedophile crackhead if you want to but when you catch something from his nasty ass don't expect me to come take you to the doctor or wipe your ass when you can't." I walked out of the front door and slammed it.

So much for coming over here to have someone to talk to. On the same day I lost Boss and Yana, I see I lost my mama too.

Chapter 3

Kit

The next morning

Escaping that trunk was the most rewarding thing I'd ever done for myself. Playing dead actually did work even though I felt very close to it at times. When the car stopped, and I remembered the latch release method I'd seen on TikTok, I got out of the trunk and went as far away as possible. The good thing was, there was an urgent care clinic very close to where I escaped. I went inside there collapsing on the floor getting immediate care at the door. After that, I don't remember much about yesterday and I didn't want to. A nigga was traumatized, to say the least.

"Excuse me." A nurse spoke over me, and I opened my eyes.

"We have the detectives here to speak with you now. Are you feeling okay?"

"Yeah, I'm good." I nodded my head attempting to clear my throat. I'd been half in and out of sleep since this morning and these pain pills had me as high as rent in Chicago.

"Ma'am, it's Detective Rainer. How are you doing today?" An officer in a grey suit and blonde buzz cut stuck his hand out in front of me.

"I'm good and you don't have to call me ma'am. I don't identify as a ma'am." I corrected him. My entire life I hated when men called me that shit. I would much rather not get their version of respect other than to feel disrespected.

"My apologies. Can I have your first and last name? I don't see it listed on our paperwork." He said, and I froze for a moment. The only reason I was here was because that sinister mutha fucka named Boss had been after me. I got away but that would only last so long until Boss found me again. That's unless he actually thought I was dead.

"I don't know my name. I can't remember it." The detective put his clipboard by his side.

"You don't remember your name?"

"No, I don't. Maybe it's the medicine."

"The nurses called us here to interview you in between any high-dosage medication being administered." He looked confused.

"Well, I don't know. I don't know my name and I can't remember anything else about myself. Y'all may as well come back another day. I'm of no good use." I replied, and the officer tucked his bottom lip. You could see from the look on his face that he didn't believe me. He shouldn't though. I was telling a flat-out lie.

"I guess we will be back maybe tomorrow to speak with you and find out who put you here. Have a good day." He replied, walking out of the door.

He could come back tomorrow but I wasn't going to say anything then either. Right now, I felt safer than I have in a minute laid up in this hospital bed, unknown, and for the moment unafraid.

Chapter 4

Boss

Two weeks later

I had Lump's ass in the air, and I was taking out my frustrations on her pussy. She already showed me a positive pregnancy test, so I wasn't worried about getting her pregnant right now. I had free range to fill her up to the rim if I wanted to with no consequences.

"Mmhmm, take this dick."

"Yes, daddy. Yes!" Lump cried out with no care in the world.

"That's right, don't move. You wanted it. Now take it. Take this dick."

I held her ass in place.

When she collapsed onto the bed, I slapped her ass and kissed up her spine.

"We not done yet, arch your back," I demanded and she listened.

When Lump curved her back like the letter C it only took about fifteen strokes before I was shooting nut on her ass. I climbed off of her and sat on the side of the bed grabbing everything I wore over here from the floor.

"Damn baby, you're leaving so quickly like you have a wife at home."

"Nah, I don't, but I do have to get my daughter tonight. Don't you have to get up early in the morning anyway?"

"Yes, unfortunately, I do." She smacked her lips before getting up and going to the restroom. Lump had an appointment for her abortion at seven in the morning and I could tell she was pissed that I suggested she do it. Her ass was only like two minutes pregnant and I damn sure wasn't trying to have two baby mamas in this world if one is not Megan. Every baby mama won't follow the code like Yana has. She was a baby mama from heaven if you asked me and next time, I may not be so lucky.

"How much is the lil procedure again?"

"$500." She replied as I walked into the restroom. She had her work uniform hanging on the back of the door and the water running for a shower.

"Alright, I'll give you more than that." I pulled out a stack of money and thumbed out two thousand dollars.

"Now I want you to call me as soon as you're ready to get picked up."

"Why won't you just drive me there and wait for me in the parking lot."

"That's too early baby and I'm too impatient to wait like that. Take an Uber and I'll pick you up when you're ready."

"You promise?"

"Of course, I promise. Call me when you're done." I reached down to kiss her on the cheek.

"But I'm about to roll. I'll hit you when I get home."

"Okay, you better." She guided my chin with her fingers to kiss her lips. We kissed for a good minute until loud knocks came to her front door. We both looked at each other at the same time but Shawty looked scared, I was more curious.

"You not going to see who that is banging on your door?"

"No."

"Why not?"

"Because I know who it is."

"It's a nigga?"

"Probably." She shrugged her shoulders. I walked towards the door, and she tried to pull me back, but I snatched away from her.

When I swung the door open, I saw it was a short stocky ass nigga in a too-little shirt looking up at me with pure hate in his eyes.

"What the fuck do you want?" I asked him and he looked past me to Lump.

"This bitch knows what I want. She is my wife!"

"Darryl not anymore! How long have we been separated?" She asked and I started to laugh.

"Lil nigga get the fuck away from this door before I shoot you."

"They didn't stop making guns when they made yours." He got fly at the mouth. I pulled out my gun and put it to his head.

"You trying to die today?"

He started to laugh like shit was funny.

"Oh, I know you. This all makes sense. Inmate." His chest swole up.

"It's Sergeant Yates. One of the men who used to tell your ass what to do seven days a week. Serenity never took my last name, so I know you never connected us there. Oh, and I don't have my dreads anymore either, but I do remember you though."

It finally made sense who he was and why he was being a dick even with a gun to his head. Sergeant Yates was at the prison when I first got there. By the time Lump showed up, he had moved facilities.

"You were pussy in that uniform and you sure as hell a pussy now."

"Serenity this is what you resort to. A violent ex-criminal who will be back in jail in no time since he's so gun-happy." He looked back at me.

"I'm fist happy too. I'll beat your ass and then shoot you."

"I know you will. That's usually what criminals do."

He said the last smart thing to me that I would take, and I punched him down to the ground. When I stood over him, I punched him several more times not stopping until I saw blood.

"Please stop Boss, I promise you, he is not worth it! We aren't together! We're getting a divorce. I don't get why he can't understand that!" She yelled and I finally stopped beating the nigga ass.

"Well understand this. I'll catch a body in two seconds about my respect, so don't witness no murder because you can't keep your husband in line."

"About to be ex-husband, Boss. Please, believe me, baby!" She pleaded as he laid unconscious on the ground.

I was still not satisfied but I couldn't kill him right now if I wanted to. Our time will come soon enough if he keeps dancing around my trigger finger.

"Whatever Lump, I'm out this bitch. Let me know when you get your shit in order." I stepped over his body and left the apartment. I could see now this shit wouldn't last long. Lump having an ex-husband just brought her stock down even more. Especially an ex-husband like fuck ass Yates.

The next morning

When Steez called my phone this early I was hoping it was for a good reason.

"What up?" I asked, leaving out of the restroom where I had Adayah in the tub.

"Just calling to tell you there's still no word. That little lead we got about her being at Medical hasn't panned out."

"Did you describe what she looked like?"

"Yeah, down to the titties. They all saying they don't know. We better of going up to the hospitals instead of talking to them bitches on the phone."

"Man, that bitch somewhere talking, I'm telling you."

"Bro, if she was, we would've been in police custody by now. That bitch is somewhere dead or in a coma. Not too many people can survive them, Lugers"

"True," I replied.

"So, check this out, what I'm going to do is send some white bitches I know to every hospital around this mutha fucka. Get them to code switch on they ass and get information they wouldn't give a nigga over the phone."

"Yeah, do that. Shit, at this point we have to do anything to find her. Even if she's dead we need her body." I replied, just as Adayah called me from the restroom.

"Daddy!"

"What lil mama?"

"I need some more bubbles."

"Steez, I'll hit you back later. Keep me posted if you hear anything."

"Alright, one." He replied before we hung up the phone.

This being a full-time daddy thing was hard ass work. Between me and my mama Adayah had us on the move. With her other grandma at the hospital with Yana, me and my mama really had to step up. I take my hat off to the mothers that make it look easy because this shit really ain't. Dealing with her requires constant attention.

"Time to get out and put on your clothes anyway mama. Your little hands getting wrinkled." I grabbed a towel from the towel rack. After drying her off, I wrapped the robe I bought her around her body.

I took her into my bedroom and helped her put on her clothes and shoes I got her from Target. I wish I had time to get her better shit, but she was cute as hell in this cheap shit. My baby didn't need Gucci to look good even though she would have plenty of it in the future.

"Where are you two going?" My mama stuck her head in the door. She hated the circumstances we were in, but she loved the fact that we were here. When Mrs. Tracey sent her from the hospital with me, I knew I wasn't going anywhere with her but to my mama's house. She's been waiting to have a grandbaby anyway. When I brought Adayah in here, she didn't ask any questions and accepted her. I wish Megan could've done the same.

"Muffin, tell grandma where we are going."

"To get some donuts! I'm hungry." She exclaimed, making us both laugh at her excitement. I was stressed out dealing with the task of fatherhood but having a daughter also gave me a feeling I couldn't explain. When she was happy, it made me happy, so I had to keep a smile on her face.

"I wish I had known y'all were going out for donuts. I was making breakfast for you two."

"Sorry, mama. She made me promise to get her donuts this morning if she went to sleep last night." I pinched her on her cheek. The discipline part of our relationship was nonexistent because I was walking on eggshells to keep her mind off of Yana.

"Well okay, y'all be safe and be back for lunch. I'll make you two some fried chicken and macaroni."

"Okay, mama," I replied before kissing her on her cheek and picking up Adayah to leave out of the house.

I had the music in the car playing but not too loud since Adayah wanted to watch her iPad. The sounds of Peppa The Pig and Cry for YOU by Jodeci took over the car and I couldn't help but think about Megan. I hadn't heard from my shawty in a week, and I missed her like a mutha fucka. I can be G enough to admit I fucked up with her but that didn't mean I ain't want her back. That was still a high priority after making sure my daughter was straight for now.

When Peppa the Pig stopped and ringing started, I turned to see what Adayah was doing.

"Lil mama, who are you calling?"

"I'm calling my mommy. Is she still getting her hair done Daddy?" She repeated the story me and Tracy came up with. Yana was doing okay, but she had a long road to recovery with the bullets piercing her lungs. It may be a month before she gets out of there.

"Huh, Daddy? Is mommy done?" She snapped me out of my head once again.

"I don't know baby. I'll have to call and check with Grandma."

"Okay, because I really miss my mama, and I want her daddy." She sounded sad as shit.

Her little voice and the pressure of not knowing what to say had a nigga wanting to kill the hoe that shot my baby mama. I hated this shit for my daughter.

"It's okay lil mama. Daddy going to get you two donuts, okay?"

"Okay, daddy. I just really wish I could share one with my mommy. Her loves donuts."

"What about sharing one with Aunt Megan?" That idea popped up in my head. From what Yana told me, Adayah loved Megan.

"Yes, I want to see her daddy. Can TT Meg come with us?" She clapped in excitement.

"Hold on, we will see." I grabbed my phone and dialed up her number. I hadn't called her in a couple of days, and I'm surprised it's still ringing. She hadn't blocked me yet.

When the line picked up, Megan let out a deep sigh.

"What do you want Boss?"

"Listen, I know you don't want to hear from me, but this isn't about me." I turned the music up so Adayah couldn't hear what I was saying.

"Adayah wants to see you because she misses her mama. I'm doing everything I can to keep her happy, but she needs to see familiar faces. She said she wants to see you." She sighed again and smacked her lips.

"Where is Tracey?"

"At the hospital with Yana." The line got quiet.

"Her and I are going to the Stan's donuts. I can come get you if you're home."

"I'm not."

"Oh, you at your mama's house?"

"No."

"Then where the fuck you at?"

"I'm at home boy damn. But I don't need a ride. I know where Stan's Donuts is."

"So, you're coming?"

"Yeah, only for her." She replied and then hung up the phone.

"She's coming, baby. Now let me see you smile."

She flashed her little teeth in the rear-view mirror. I hope this was a step in the right direction to get my bitch back. I know just seeing her in person could change a lot. It always did.

Once I pulled up to the donut shop, I parked up front and got Adayah out the back. She cheered up quickly seeing the statue of the donut outside with sprinkles just like the one she asked for. As soon as we were walking in, I heard a car alarm chirp and spotted Megan walking towards us with her hands in her jacket pocket.

"Look who it is." I got Adayah's attention.

"TT Meg." She ran up to her. Megan bent down and hugged her tightly before holding her face.

"You, okay?"

"Yes, I'm okay. I'm about to get donuts!"

"I know, I'm happy for you mama. I missed you."

She replied, flashing my daughter a smile. I wanted her to look at up me and smile the same way, but I instead got the cold shoulder. She held hands with Adayah and acted as if I wasn't there.

We walked into the shop and Adayah instantly started pointing at the pink donut with sprinkles behind the glass.

"Welcome to Stan's Donuts, how can I help you?"

"Yeah, I need two of those pink sprinkle donuts and two glazed ones. Which kind do you want?" I asked Megan.

"None, I'm fine. I haven't been eating much. No appetite."

She had a nigga feeling bad as fuck. Even though she was still fine as shit, she looked like she hadn't slept in days. Her hair was in a ponytail, and there were small bags under her eyes.

"Well, that's it for now. Oh, add a water too." I replied, before swiping my card.

Once we got our donuts and water we sat at the table and Adayah started eating, I was unable to not address what was going on between Megan and me.

"Fox, I didn't mean to keep things from you I swear. We just didn't know how to tell you. Yana wanted to but."

"But you didn't. You wanted to have your cake and eat it too like always." She rolled her eyes.

"That's not true. I didn't want you to get hurt. I know how much you wanted a kid, and I ain't want you to feel a way because I had one without you." She lifted her hand to shut me up.

"I don't want to talk about it, Boss. I'm just here for her, that's it." She snapped, and I left her alone. I wasn't giving up on her, just like I didn't the last time. Just her being here right now was good enough for me. I knew I was going to have to work to get her back and I wasn't afraid of that challenge. I had to do this same shit before.

Chapter 5

Megan

How much can one woman take? How stupid could I be? I was sitting in the donut shop with a man that has a baby by my best friend. I had so many questions I wanted to ask him, but I was scared to know any answers. The more details I get about their betrayal, the more the shit will probably hurt.

"TT, I have to go to the restroom," Adayah spoke up after biting her donut.

"Okay, I'll take you. Come on." I stood up from the table and led her to the restrooms. When I got her in a stall and wrapped the toilet seat for her, my phone rang from my pocket.

"Mrs. Sanchez?" I spoke out loud seeing Kit mama's name on my ID. She was in an old folk's home, crippled and half ass crazy. I didn't go see her much, but I made sure to stop by on holidays. Kit however went to see her mama at least once a week.

"Hey, Mrs. Sanchez," I answered the phone.

"Hello, Megan. How are you doing?"

"I'm okay just making it. How about yourself?"

"I'm as good as one can be with my health. Can I speak to my daughter? I need her to go ahead and sign these papers so that I can sell my house since she has power of attorney over me. I'm not living there anyway and with the money I get from the sale I can move into a better facility."

She replied, as Adayah hopped up from the toilet seat and I sighed hoping to break this as easily as possible.

"Mrs, Sanchez, Kit and I are not together anymore. We've been broken up for some time now."

"Oh, I didn't realize that."

"Yes ma'am. So, I really don't know where she is. I'm sorry."

"Well does she have her phone? I've been calling her for days and she hasn't answered."

"I'm really not sure. As I said I haven't spoken with her in a while. She will most likely be calling you back soon though."

"Yeah, or maybe she won't, and I'll have to bury another child. I just don't have a good feeling about her missing like this." She started to speak negatively which is the usual since she was medically prescribed Xanax.

"Mrs. Sanchez just stay calm, and I'm sure you will hear from her soon. I have to go now but take care of yourself."

"Okay, thank you, baby. Bye." She replied and hung up the phone. When we came out of the restroom Boss was sitting at the table looking down at his phone. I was trying not to look at him right now because I didn't want my mind to tell me to lust over him. I did however have a few questions to ask him since Kit was missing. Knowing Boss, he could be the very reason for that.

"I just got off the phone with Kit's mom and she's missing."

"Okay, and?" He shrugged his shoulder before biting into his last donut.

"And I want to know what you did to her."

"I didn't do anything to her but had I, it would've been deserved. The bitch did put a hit out on me." He spoke so nonchalantly that I couldn't tell if he was lying or not.

"Well anyway, I'm going to leave now. It was so good seeing you TT baby." I hugged and kissed Adayah on the cheek.

"Wait, please don't go." She pleaded, holding on to my sweatshirt.

"I'm sorry baby, I have to."

"Well, can you at least take me to my mama? Her still getting her hair done and I miss her."

I looked at Boss who didn't really know what to say just as I didn't. The look on her face however had me in fix-it mode. This poor baby is innocent even if her parents were backstabbing conniving ass mutha fuckas.

"How about a sleepover with me at my house?"

"Yay! That sounds fun!" She cheered while jumping up and down.

When I thought about it, I didn't want her there because of my insane-ass ex-girlfriend popping up, so I came up with a better idea.

"How about we stay at a hotel instead? One with a pool on the inside and your daddy will pay for it."

She got even more excited and when I looked at Boss he had a smile on his face. It wasn't my goal to make him smile because I didn't really care how he felt. It would take a lot more for me to care about his feelings. Until then I was focusing on myself and what makes me happy

"Your neck hurting again?" Boss asked, noticing I was rubbing the back of my neck.

"Yep, stressed out of course."

"Do you want to get a massage? My treat?"

"I can pay for my massage if I want one, Boss."

"I know you can but as long as I'm living, I don't want you to spend any of your own money. It's all on me so find a hotel with a spa too."

"Whatever." I shrugged my shoulders and took my conversation back to the baby.

"You ready to go my love?"

"Yeah, daddy, are you going too?" She asked Boss and I felt a burning sensation in my heart. Loving this baby couldn't take away the pain I felt when I heard her call him daddy. It was like hearing it for the first time over and over again.

"No, he's not going. Let's go." I got up from the table and walked Adayah to my car.

Boss was behind us every step of the way and when I went to put her in the backseat he grabbed my arm.

"Wait, let me get her booster seat and her outfits and shit out the trunk." he jogged to his car and grabbed all of her stuff.

When he came back with the bags and the seat, I got even more irritated.

"Good to see you have your own booster seat now. You not hiding it in your trunk anymore?"

"Megan, I never hid it in my trunk. I didn't have one."

"Oh yeah, because you were being a deadbeat dad once you got out of prison to keep up with a lie, got it." I snatched the seat and put it into my car.

"Megan, I understand you're mad at me, but I promise you, this shit wasn't supposed to happen this way. That night you and her told me to come fuck y'all, I didn't expect to get her pregnant."

"But you did. You did and you kept it from me instead of telling me the truth!"

"Why would I have told you, Megan, you would've reacted the same way regardless!"

"You don't know that! You can predict my reactions to anything! You hid her because you wanted to do shit behind my back!" I punched him in the chest. It didn't seem to faze him though.

"Baby! Listen to me!" Boss's grip tightened on my arms. He pulled me so close that our breaths became one, in the narrow space between us.

"I understand that you're mad and I can't change that, but you know who I wanted a child with. That shit was an accident, and I'll let you have your ill feelings for now but eventually, I need you to get over this shit." He looked down at me with knitted eyebrows almost convincing me to listen. It took everything in me to not fall into the trap of hanging on to his every word like I used to.

"Move, Boss!" I matched his facial expression and pushed him off me.

"I'm about to go to the hotel so you can send me the money." I rolled my eyes and got in my car. I was anxious to get away from Boss because being around him right now was too much. My emotions were all over the place.

I booked the most expensive room I could at the Ritz Carlton hotel which ran Boss $1500 for one night. We went up to the room and I opened the door, and Adayah went crazy over the view.

"We can see everything from up here TT! Thank you for bringing me here!" She hugged my leg.

"Don't thank me, thank your-." I stopped speaking because it was hard for me to say her dad. She ignored my stutter and ran to look out the floor-to-ceiling windows and I sat down on the bed and kicked my boots off.

I got undressed down to my panties and turned the television on for Adayah in the living area. When I walked past the door to go to the restroom, I heard knocking and quickly grabbed a robe from the closet nearby.

"Just one second!"

"Who is it!" I yelled after getting myself together.

"It's room service." I heard the voice that popped up on me more than anyone else. This nigga followed us here anyway.

"Boss, what are you doing here?"

I asked after opening the door.

"What do you mean? My woman and my daughter are here."

"Hi, Daddy!" Adayah yelled from the couch.

"My question is, how did you know where we were?"

"Adayah's brand-new iPad. You know Find My iPhone is a thing now, right?"

"And how did you get our room number?"

"To be honest, I flirted with the clerk all while telling her I wanted to surprise my wife and daughter here." I crossed my arms.

"Boss that's not fair, you know I said I didn't want you here."

"Yeah, you said that, but how does she feel?" He rubbed his hands in between my legs. He walked towards the bed and sat down looking out the window at Chicago from a view I could tell he wasn't used to. Boss was from the depths of Chicago. The gritty, unruly, Southside that grew babies into monsters. Right now, at this moment, Boss was stuck admiring something he found beautiful that wasn't a bitch. In the hood he grew up in, that was a rare occurrence and made him so small-minded.

"It's beautiful right?" I walked up beside him.

"It doesn't matter, I won't see it for long. I'm getting put out of here, right?" He looked at me with a twinkle in his hazel eyes. Handsome, just couldn't quite describe him.

"Well, we are getting put out too once you stop paying for this room."

"I won't stop until you want me to." He licked his lips, and I shook my head. Handsome and slick I may add.

"Anyway, I was going to get in the shower, so you can find your way out now." I walked into the restroom.

After starting the water, I heard Boss talking to Adayah in the other room.

"Alright. Don't come to this door until Daddy comes back out, okay?" He said, coming into the bathroom and closing the doors.

"Boss, what are you doing? I told you to leave."

"I know, but I want to make it up to you. I know words can only say so much to the ears, so I have to get your forgiveness through your skin, through touch." He wrapped his arms around my waist and backed me up against the counter.

He started to kiss my neck near the front of my collarbone which he knew was my special spot.

"I promise I'll leave after this. Just let me take care of you." He lifted me to the counter. I was already undressed so Boss kissed down in between my legs and slid my panties to the side before vacuuming my clit into his mouth.

His tongue flicked from side to side over my clit so forcefully that the pressure made me want to scream. I covered my mouth with my hand and bit my lip as much as possible with him in between my thighs.

When I looked down and saw him going in on my pussy I quickly closed my eyes trying not to cum. That did nothing but make it worse because I started visualizing what he was doing to me.

My thighs began to tremble, and he felt me near my peak, so he took his mouth off my center and stood up to kiss me on my lips. Boss had so much of my nectar on his lips that I knew exactly what I tasted like, and I was scrumptious if I may add.

Boss kissed back down to my pussy and this time I was even more sensitive than before. Once he started licking fast circles around my clit, that was all she wrote. I squirted all over the restroom counters and some on his lips putting a grin on his face.

"Fu, uh, uck." I panted as Boss stood up smiling. His hand was in his pants and seconds later he was pulling his dick out to shoot nut in the toilet.

"Nobody told you to get yours, nigga." I rolled my eyes jumping down from the counter.

"Why not? Your pussy is too sweet not to." He replied, grabbing the complimentary toothbrush and toothpaste from the counter.

"I planned on using that you know I didn't bring any stuff here."

"Just order what you need. I told you I got you." He started to brush his teeth. Trying to ignore his presence I went into the shower doors and got lost under the soothing waters. Boss brushed his teeth for a few minutes and then shut the water off.

"Alright, I'm about to leave, I'll see y'all later." He shouted over the shower water.

"Bye Boss and don't pop up over here again. I swear I will leave y'all here."

"Whatever you say, mama."

He replied because he thought shit was sweet. I may have let him eat my pussy just now, but I had to stop it there. God knows I wanted to be done with this man and I'm tired of being caught inside this toxic ass maze of love with him.

Chapter 6
Lump

When I woke up and heard Darryl snoring from the living room I rolled my eyes. How his divorcing me turned into him on my couch was beyond me.

After Boss knocked him out, I felt bad, so I dragged him inside the apartment, and he laid on the floor unconscious for a good ten minutes. I knew calling the ambulance would get Boss arrested so I waited until he came too. Darryl was so out of it that he sat on my couch, laid back, and went to sleep once again. I hoped his stupid ass has a concussion after what he did last night.

Before leaving out of my room I put my robe on and tied it extra tight around my waist. When I walked out of the room, I went into the kitchen thinking he was asleep until I felt his hand around the back of my neck.

"So, you have been fucking inmates this whole time! Bitch you thought you were getting away with that."

"I have not been fucking inmates. I've been doing my job and Boss is not an inmate anymore." He tightened the grip around my neck.

"Yeah, you say that shit but is it true? I know you Serenity, and you been looking for a nigga like him for years."

"No, I haven't!"

"Yes, you have! And let me tell you, it may seem cool at first, but fucking with a man like that ain't what you want! It's not what you're used to!" He squeezed my neck a little harder.

"Do you even know this nigga? Do you know what he is about? Or do you just know he got money and jewelry and shit?"

"I don't care about what he has. I was just digging him!"

"Digging him? You mean one of the deadliest niggas in Chicago. Digging a man who had a prison full of murders and convicts scared of him. That should tell you something. You just started in this prison shit, but I been around niggas like him for years!" He pushed my head forward by the neck. I didn't reply to him because I knew from our past that he could go on and on especially when he thought he was right. I never saw a man who knew it all yet experienced so little in life. Darryl went from the military to the prison system and only moved out from with his mama when he got with me. As far as the streets and that life his ass didn't know anything other than what thugs are like in prison. He doesn't understand them niggas be in survival mode in there. I would get grimy too if I were locked up.

I walked away from Darryl, and he was on my heels following me into my room.

"Where the fuck are you going Serenity? We not done talking."

"Yes, we are, I have to leave here soon." I attempted to shut my door, but he pushed his way through.

I opened my panty drawer to get underwear and into my closet to find something comfortable to put on. I had to make it to my abortion appointment, and I had no time to argue. I would rather Darryl be pissed off with me than Boss.

"You going to see that nigga ain't you? I know you not working today since you grabbed that wired bra." He noticed what was in my hand. Trust and believe Sargent Yates knew the ends and outs of the prison uniform rules.

"Nigga, I'm going to the gym to workout. And I don't have to answer to you anyway!" He shook his head as if he was frustrated with me

"Yeah, but you're not about to be with nobody else either. I said we needed time apart. Not for you to be fucking around in the streets!"

"Darryl, you filed for divorce because you're insecure as hell! So please leave me alone before I get my new man to come back over here. I know you don't want to deal with him again."

I snapped, only causing Darryl to get even more mad. He pushed me down to the floor and started to punch me with all the strength he had. He pulled my hair and dragged me around the living room like I was some type of rag doll.

Once he was finally done beating on me, he spit on me and kicked me in the back like I was nothing.

"Now excuse me. I have to go to work and find an excuse as to why my nose is broken. Now you'll have to do the same when you go back." He walked out of my bedroom.

After a few seconds, I could hear the front door slam, so I knew he'd finally left. When I got up to go grab tissue for my nose I felt an uncomfortable wetness form in between my legs. I figured I peed on myself during this beating, so I went into the room to take off these clothes. When I pulled down my pants, I saw a spot of blood in my panties.

"Oh, my God. This nigga must've killed the baby." I placed my hand over my mouth. Even though I was about to get an abortion in a couple of hours, I would still never forgive him for what he just did.

Later that day

The bleeding had subsided earlier today, and I was unfortunately on my way to work. I hated that at the prison we could only call off so many days before being fired. I see why Darryl wanted me to get a job here because it put me in prison too. For twelve hours out of the day, I was locked up with no life, no phone, no real friends. I may as well be an inmate too because my life was in a box. I liked the money, but the lifestyle was still too much for me.

Darryl's attack had only left marks on the back of my neck which I covered up with a turtleneck. I was a pro at covering up my eyes from our relationships so you couldn't tell that I'd ever been touched. I went through the first gate and into the building with my head held high and my nose turned up. Nothing or no one was interfering with my pride in here today. I'd already been physically beaten down enough.

When I got to my post in pod A, it was time to do count. We yelled for everyone to step out of their cell doors so that we could start it up. When I got halfway down my block another guard named Jeffers walked up to me.

"Lumpkins, I'll take over for you. Warden Francis wants you in her office."

"In her office for what?"

"I don't know." She shrugged her shoulders, and I handed her the counting clicker.

"Get your asses outside these doors and whoever isn't standing straight up is getting a write-up. Do not lean!" I listened to Jeffers yell at the guards as I walked away.

Once I got down the hallway to her office I knocked twice, and she asked who it was over the intercom.

"It's Lumpkins, you wanted to see me?"

"Yes, come in." She unlocked the door. I didn't expect to be greeted with a smile because Francis wasn't the type, but I sure as hell didn't expect her to have a mug on her face.

"Hello, Warden." I nervously spoke to her.

"You can have a seat." She directed me. I knew I wasn't getting fired because any time a firing happens there has to be witnesses.

"Do you know why I called you here?" She asked, clasping her hands together on the desk.

"No, I don't. I was wondering what it could be."

She took a deep breath.

"You know Lumpkins when you started here, I had high hopes for you being the wife of one of our best Sergeants. It hurt me to see him transfer units, but he spoke very highly of you and your work ethic. You graduated from Chicago State University, correct?"

"Yes."

"Smart girl then. I would think a lot smarter than someone who would get caught up with a monster like Boss the Killa as he's known on the streets." She caught me off guard.

"Listen, I don't know what Darryl told you but I'm sure none of it is true. I did not start talking to him here. That's the God-honest truth."

"Sergeant Yates didn't tell me anything. My private detective did. He's been following Boss around for about two weeks and we see now that he doesn't live a righteous lifestyle." She got up to walk around the table.

"Lumpkins, I want you to understand that judges do not care whether you like a man, they don't care how much money he spent on you, or how the man sexed you like crazy." She shook her head from side to side.

"You will get just as much time as he does if you are involved with anything illegal that he's doing. That's whether you know about his endeavors, or if you're simply just around." She went back to her seat.

"Warden Francis Boss hasn't done anything illegal around me. We are seeing each other but that's it."

"That's it?"

"That's it."

She pressed her lips firmly together.

"Well, okay. If you say so Lumpkins, you may go back to your post now." She shooed her hands to the door.

When I got up to leave, she stopped me once more before I could leave out of the door.

"When Boss's world comes crashing down on his head you need to be, far far away from him."

"Okay, thanks for the heads up. I'll be sure to cut him off." I replied before I walked out of her office. My heart was still beating, and my head was even more fucked up than it was when I walked into this prison earlier.

From the way Francis was speaking, Boss wouldn't be a free man for long. That's if her mean ass could help it.

Chapter 7

Kit

The police came back to my room twice and I was already tired of saying that I didn't know anything. Since I wasn't telling them my name, they came up with the idea to get a fingerprint from me to run through the system. I agreed to it, so now I knew I had to run.

When the nurses did their last check for the night, I knew it was my time to go. I didn't have extra clothes here, so I put on my extra nightgown in the back and tied the dresses to stay in place on the side. When I walked out of the hospital room, no one was at the nurse's station, and I noticed a black jacket hanging on the back of a chair. I grabbed it and put it on before taking the hood over my head and going onto the elevator.

I was moving slowly, but I was still moving nonetheless. I made it all the way outside before I had my first regret about leaving the hospital. It was cold as shit out here, so I hugged my body tightly to avoid the brutal wind.

I know the safest place I could go to get money to skip town was to my mama. I didn't plan on staying around Chicago for long because I knew if I did, I would be shot again.

When I spotted the bus stop about fifty yards away. I knew I needed to find cash first to get to the nursing home. I turned around searching the parking lot for people until I saw a white lady walking out to her car. Her LGBQT decal in the back window made me feel comfortable to ask her because we all usually looked out for each other.

"Excuse me, ma'am." I caught up to her.

"Yes?"

"Do you happen to have a couple of dollars so that I can catch the bus? I'm just now getting discharged, and I have no way to get home."

"I don't carry cash, sorry."

"Okay. Thank you, Miss," I replied walking away from her. Before I could get too far, she was calling me back.

"Hey, where you going? I can give you a ride if it's not too far out."

"To my mama's retirement facility. It's near 55th Street."

"Okay, hop in. I'll take you." She kept towards her car.

"Oh, and just to let you know, I do have a gun. And I will use it if I have to."

"Ma'am, I promise I'm not on that type of time. I just need a ride away from here."

"Okie dokie."

She hit the unlock button on the keypad and we got in her car.

"What's the name of the retirement home again?"

"Sunset Retirement Home."

She put that name into the GPS, and it said we were 17 minutes away. She drove off towards the home and I attempted to make small talk so she wouldn't be nervous being next to a complete stranger.

"I really appreciate the ride. You from Chicago?"

"Yeah, born and raised. What about you?"

"Same, but I would love to get away from here one day. I can't stand this place."

"Well coming from someone who's gotten away, this place is no different than the rest of the world. Chicago is just more known for its bad than other cities."

"That's true," I replied, and we went silent for a minute until she decided to keep the conversation going.

"So, what's your name?"

"My name is Kitina, or Kit as some call me. What about you?"

"I'm Candice, or Candy to my friends."

"Am I your friend?"

"Not, yet." She looked at me and winked her eyes. Was she feeling me or sum?

"Do you have family here, Candy?"

"No, it's just me in this big-ass city by myself. My mom and dad used to live here before they both died. I have family all over the country. Don't see them often though."

"That sucks, sorry to hear that."

"No, it doesn't suck, I'm okay with it. I have that kind of family that is better at a distance. I couldn't imagine answering the door and my aunt being on my steps."

"Yeah, annoying relatives is the worst." We both laughed.

"How old are you if you don't mind me asking?"

"I'm thirty-two years young, nowhere near forty thank God, I still have a little youth in me." She grabbed a cigarette from her middle console. She put it up to her lips to light it and then stopped.

"Wait, were you inside the hospital for lung problems?"

"No, not at all, just had a few bumps and bruises that needed tending too. You are straight though. Do what you gotta do."

She smirked and put the cigarette up to her lighter.

"You know, I can't tell you smoke in here. I didn't smell the smoke when I got in, and I know how strong it used to have my grandma's car smelling."

"Yeah, I don't smoke in here unless I've had a long day. Today just happened to be one of those."

"Really, what happened?"

"Honestly, anytime I'm at the hospital it's a bad day. My friend has lupus and I'm the only person who checks on her."

"Damn."

"Yeah, and this visit tonight fucked me up. She looks worse than she ever has. I really don't know what I'm going to do without her."

She got quiet and so did I because I instantly started thinking about Dezzy. My nigga didn't get a second chance at life like me and it devastated me to know I made a mistake by killing him. Thinking about that day hurt worse than any bullet that hit my body. I reacted off anger instead of knowledge, I knew that wasn't Dezzy's doing but at the time I wanted someone to blame.

"You know Candy, I lost my best friend a few weeks ago and I can tell you, it hurts like a mutha fucker. I can however say that every day it gets a little easier. You just have to take it day by day."

"You're right. You're so so right." She tilted her head and smiled. I made her happy but now I was catching a falling tear from my eye overcome with emotions of my own.

"You mind if I have one of those cigarettes," I asked, hoping to cope with my sadness before it took over me.

"Of course, have at it." She replied, handing me the box along with a lighter. I lit a cigarette and inhaled it slowly because I'd never been a tobacco smoker before. Surprisingly, it calmed me down and slowly dried up the tears attempting to fall because of Dezzy.

When we pulled in front of the building, she put her car in park, and I unfastened my seatbelt.

"I really appreciate you for bringing me here. You didn't have to, but you did."

"Of course I did, it was no problem at all new friend." She smiled at me.

When I went to grab the door handle, it was suddenly pulled from the outside, and standing in front of me was Steez, Boss's right-hand man and number one hitch-man.

"Candy Girl, you just earned a bonus. I knew we would find her ass." He put his gun up to my chest.

"It was easy Steez baby, she literally fell into my lap."

"Bitch! You set me up!"

I said, being wrestled out of the front seat.

"Oh well, you fuckin dummy."

She replied, before pulling off and laughing cut the window. What are the fucking odds that I would end up getting a ride to my death.

Steez and Ahmad threw me into the back of an SUV, and they quickly tied my hands up. Before I could get a scream out, they were duct-taping my mouth shut and making me feel as if I couldn't breathe. I wasn't well, and I shouldn't have ever left the hospital in my condition. Now I was back in the hands of these niggas. I may as well start praying now.

"Alright Steez, she secured, drive off."

"Are we sure? This bitch already got away from us once." Steez asked and Ahmad confirmed. Steez then hopped in the front seat and drove off from the retirement home to my demise.

The song playing over the speaker was interrupted by ringing and Steez quickly turned the music down.

"What's up, you paged me?" I heard Boss over the speaker,

"Yeah, we got that hoe."

"Swear to God?"

"Yeah. You know I told you I had one of my hoes Candy camped out at the hospital trying to see what she could see. She said this hoe walked up to her and texted me where to meet them."

"Alright, keep her ass alive until I get there. And don't lose her ass. I'm going to make sure she dies this time." He replied before hanging up the phone. I closed my eyes, and a tear ran down my face because hearing his voice legit put fear in my soul. That man shot me with no remorse whatsoever. At first, I can admit, I wasn't as scared of him, but now I am.

Boss is who he says he is which is everything I'm not. I should've just stuck to making money and left this street life alone. It wasn't for me after all.

Chapter 8

Megan

Adayah and I had to leave the hotel to go by my apartment so I could get some more clothes to stay another night. She was honestly a welcoming distraction to all the hurtful things constantly popping up in my head. Seeing Boss yesterday only made the situation worse because I was now craving his affection.

When we pulled into my parking spot, I didn't get that welcoming feeling you're supposed to get when you get home. I felt dread, anger, and regret about the past few years of my life here.

I helped Adayah out of the car, and we walked inside. The heater kicked on just as we entered the door, and I was happy to feel the heat after being in what felt like a blizzard outside.

I grabbed a pair of pants, a sweater, and a hoodie from the closet along with something to sleep in. I could hear Adayah on her iPad in the living room and her tiny giggles made me smile.

"You okay in there, TT baby? I'm almost done."

"Yes, I'm okay!" She continued laughing at the video. I turned off all the lights in the room and walked into the living room to grab my fast-charging phone charger when loud knocks suddenly started at my door.

Boom, Boom, Boom

I instantly got terrified. All I could think was that Kit was back and ready to kill me in front of this baby. I pulled out my phone to call Boss, and a man shouted, "Police." On the other side of the door.

"Police?" I questioned myself before walking up to the peephole. What the fuck could they have wanted unless they were here for Kit or Boss.

I opened the door, and two officers were standing in front of me.

"Yes, we are here for Megan Fox."

"This is she," I replied, crossing my arms in confusion.

"We have a warrant for your arrest. Please turn around and put your hands behind your back."

"Under arrest for what?"

"Money Laundering." He put a sick feeling in my stomach.

"You have a right to remain silent. Whatever you say can and will be held against you in the court of law." He started doing his spill and I immediately started to cry.

"What about my niece? No one is here to get her."

"We will take her to the station, and you can let us know who to contact to come and pick her up."

"I don't understand what is going on. Please just tell me what this is about?" I cried, as one of the officers escorted me out of the apartment. I was asking what this was about, but I knew what was going on. Money laundering is when you disguise illegal money as legal money to use it undetected. That was exactly what Kit, and I were doing at our shops. What she said was a foolproof plan.

When we got to the police station, I was taken into a back room where I sat alone in the cold. I could hear Adayah talking to the female officer outside when the door opened, and an officer walked in.

"Can we get a good number on who to call to get the child, Ms. Fox?"

"Yes, you can call her dad. His number is 774-768-5689." I replied and he went back out the door. I'm sure he would be upset that he had to come get her, but he wasn't half as mad as I was for being here. My mind was taking a beating and now my freedom was on the verge of being taken away too.

After the detective was gone for a while, he came back inside and sat across from me with a friendly look on his face.

"Megan, sorry to keep you waiting. Can I get you anything? A drink, coffee, water, soda?"

"No, I'm fine, thanks anyway," I replied crossing my arms.

"So, just to get to the important part because there is no need to waste each other's time. We are investigating money laundering at your hair shop, Fendi."

"Money laundering, what's that?" I played clueless.

"We were tipped off that your shop is cleaning drug money through your books, and we have found evidence that says the same."

"How would I be doing that? I don't know what you're talking about."

"Oh yes, you do."

"I don't."

"Megan, I know you do."

"How!" he and I went back and forth, and the conversation got more hostile.

"So, upon digging we've found large amounts of money being accumulated through your shop. On your website you advertise your highest services range from three to four hundred dollars, yet you were putting that you make at least ten thousand in a day some days. It's rather comical."

"And I do, my shop can't be busy?"

"And we thought about that Ms. Fox, but it doesn't add up with surveillance videos from the donut shop across the street. For instance, on March 13th you recorded that you made ten thousand dollars, but we only watched two customers come in that day. What a hell of a hairstyle they must've gotten."

"Well, we also do consultations, deposits, and yes getting black women's hair done is expensive. You wouldn't know about that because you're not black and you have no hair."

I took a shot at his appearance because he was pissing me off.

"You're right, I don't have knowledge of black women's hair, but I do know about crime and people doing things like this to cover it up. Do you realize that we have a confession and someone who has laid out everything for us? There is no need to lie, Megan, we just wanted to know if you will admit to your crimes and not go to trial."

"I'm not admitting to shit because I didn't do shit. Can I please leave here, now?"

"I'm sorry Megan but you're under arrest, you will see a judge on Monday to discuss possible bond if any. Will we be getting a confession from you? I promise it will make this situation a lot easier for you."

"Nope."

"Alright then, take care of yourself." He replied before walking out of the room and leaving me at the lowest point I'd ever been in my whole life.

Now I feel dumb for ever trusting Kit's judgment. Trusting Kit at all for that matter.

Chapter 9

Boss

I walked up to the counter at the flower shop with two bouquets in my arms for the two women who had me wrapped around their fingers. I was attempting to prove myself because I hadn't been my best self to either of them in the past.

"Can I get anything else for you?"

"No ma'am, that's it."

"Okay, $246.95" she smiled, wrapping up Adayah's flowers in pink paper. I paid while she put Megan's inside yellow paper to match her flowers. Once she was done making them look all fancy, I struggled to get both of them out the door.

"Thank you, ma'am. I appreciate it." I spoke to a woman holding the door.

When I got to my car, I had a message from Steez that read, 911. I know this nigga was getting impatient waiting on me, but I had other important shit to handle first. As long as that fuck as bitch was under wraps, I was good. He was going to have to wait a minute.

When I sat inside my driver's seat, I dialed out to Steez who was talking to me on a burner phone.

"Hello, what up nigga?" He answered on the first ring.

"What up boy. I'm leaving downtown now, and I have to make one stop first and then I will be there.

"Bruh, just let me give this bitch a headshot to not waste your time. She doesn't deserve to be breathing this long. Plus, a nigga hungry and shit. You know Mys not here to do shift changes with me."

"Bruh, I will treat you to a big ass steak when we leave there. Just hold her off for a little longer, I'm on my way. I want to make sure I'm the one that kills her. It's personal to me."

"Alright bruh, but I'm eating good tonight. I want to eat at one of them restaurants you be taking them hoes." He laughed, before hanging up the phone. I put on some music and drove to the hotel to surprise Megan and Adayah with what I had for them.

When I got around the block from them, an unfamiliar number came on my phone.

"Hello?"

"Yes, is this Isiah Grayson?"

"Yeah, this him, who is this?" I wondered who was calling me by my real name.

"This is Officer Miles at the Chicago police department. We have your daughter here."

"For what?" I tighten my grip on the phone.

"She was with Megan Fox who we just brought in on a warrant. We need you to come pick her up or someone else next of kin by 5:00 or we will have to send her to DCF."

"Nah, I'm on my way."

"Okay, just ask for Detective Miles when you get here." She replied before hanging up the phone. I made a U-turn in the street and started driving like a damn fool to the police station. What the fuck do they mean Megan got brought in on a warrant? I'm sure it has to be because of a traffic ticket or some shit. Megan's green ass doesn't do shit illegal.

Once I got to the station, I parked my car in the parking lot and ran into the building feeling myself start to sweat being around all these police. The last time I was in here it was the beginning of what I thought was the end of my life.

"I'm here to see Detective Miles, she has my daughter," I spoke to the officer at the front desk.

"Okay, I'll call her out here." She got up and went through a locked door. I stood in the lobby waiting for about five minutes before a cop and Adayah walked out of the back.

Adayah had a lollipop in her hand and she smiled brightly when she saw me.

"Well, here we are. Thank you for coming in a timely manner, Mr. Grayson. We made sure to keep her busy since she's been here. You both have a good day." She turned to walk away.

"Wait a minute." I stopped her from walking off.

"What's going on with Megan, what did she get charged with?"

"Money Laundering."

"How? That doesn't even make sense."

"I don't know sir. I guess you will have to find out in court if she doesn't take a plea deal of some sort before then. I have to go now." She walked back through the locked doors. I took Adayah to the car and sat there for a minute before pulling off with my stomach in mutha fuckin knots. How did Megan end up in this type of trouble? The only thing I could think of was dealing with that dumb-ass bitch Kit who thought she was the smartest mutha fucka in the world with no street smarts. If she got Megan caught up, I was going to kill her even slower.

I rode in silence thinking about what could've happened until an epiphany hit me out of nowhere.

"They said they were cleaning money through her shop! I knew that shit was dumb as fuck!" I spoke out loud.

"What's wrong Daddy?"

"Nothing is wrong mama. I'm about to take you to your grandma's house real quick."

"Grandma Tracy?"

"No grandma, Paula. Daddy got some business to handle." I replied, and she started to whine in the backseat. She would get to know my mama soon enough and I'm sure my mama will win her over at some point. I couldn't cater to her little wants and whining right now.

After Dropping Adayah off to my mama, I drove out west to the warehouse we had that bitch at.

I put my car in park and then got ready to step out before I was stopped by another call.

It showed up as Cook County Jail and I knew it was Megan, so I answered the phone quickly.

"You have a collect call from, Megan, at the Cook County jail." She spoke, and I immediately hit accept on her call. The phone went silent for just a few moments before Megan was on the phone crying in my ear.

"Boss, I'm in jail!"

"Baby just calm down, everything is going to be okay, I'm going to make sure you're straight."

"Boss, I can't be in here like this. I'm not made for this shit."

"And you won't be. We will get you out soon. Stop crying, mama."

"They are saying that someone is cooperating with them on the case. I know it's Kit telling them all this shit."

She confirmed what I already knew.

"Don't say another word and just know that I got you. I'm going to get this shit straight for you and that's a promise." I replied to her over the phone.

"Call me back again tonight if they let you. When are they saying you will be going to court?"

"Not until Monday."

"Okay, well that's just two days away baby. Hold your head up and when you get a bond, I'm getting you out. That's a promise."

"Okay." She sniffled into the phone.

"I love you, Megan."

"I love you too, Boss."

"Talk to you later."

"Okay."

She replied and hung up the phone. I jumped straight out of the car with a mission hearing Megan crying like that. Trust I've been inside of prison and it's nothing anyone could ever really get used to. Thank God I had the remedy for this problem in my possession as we speak.

When I walked into the warehouse, I could hear the sound of Eminem playing which was Steez's favorite artist.

"About time you came through nigga. I been itching to kill this bitch."

"Yeah, my bad bruh, I been dealing with something major."

Kit opened her eyes, and they started to gloss over while staring at me. I reached to take off the tape from her mouth, "I wouldn't do that if I were you. That dumb ass bitch screams just like a female."

"She not going to say a fuckin word. She bet not."

I replied, pulling the tape off her mouth.

"Look up at me!" I demanded as soon as she dropped her head.

"Why the fuck is Megan in jail for money laundering right now! You snitched on my bitch?"

She didn't say a word and I wanted to rock this bitch chin, but before I did, I asked her one more time. I didn't want to hit a woman and Shorty was indeed a female.

"Did you go to the police on my bitch?"

"That's what I was trying to tell you when you shot me like you were putting down an animal."

"You will see a real animal if you don't tell me what you told the police about Megan."

"I was mad! That girl played me, and I wanted her ass to suffer so I told them about our little scheme at our shops. How we were cleaning money."

"Well, you're about to tell them that you doing that shit by yourself."

"For what? You're about to kill me anyway so just do it. Let Megan deal with her karma on her own." She talked her shit wearing down on my thinned patience.

"Listen, you going to the police, tell them that you were lying, and getting Megan's name out of this shit."

"For what? Why would I do that? What does it benefit me?"

"You get to live. If you do anything sneaky once I get you in front of the police, I'm killing you, your mama, and anybody else you love but I'm going to make your life a living hell before I smoke you. Try me and you will see just how much of an animal I really am. Even your blood won't be enough"

I replied, then walked away from her to make a phone call. There were always ways out of trouble with the police and I'm proof of that. My bitch won't be spending any years in jail because I would burn this whole city down first before I let that happen.

Chapter 10

Lump

The next night

When I called the unit Darryl works at, they said he was there on his night shift so I knew he wouldn't be coming to bother me tonight. I'd told Boss to come over to talk and he was supposed to be over here hours ago. I'd cleaned my place up from top to bottom and put fresh sheets on my bed. I purchased all the ingredients to make a nice beef stew and had that simmering the entire night. I was a homemaker at heart and a damn good wife if my husband is someone who deserves it. I want to spoil Boss and show him that side of Serenity. As good as his dick is, I know he would bring out the best version of me. That's if he held up to his part of the relationship.

The clock read 12:30 am and I was past irritated waiting for him to show up. I got my phone, dialed his number only jumping when I heard someone knocking at my door. I checked the peephole to make sure it wasn't Darryl and smiled when I saw it was my boo. Only I had to wipe the smile off of my face because I had to give him some type of attitude for being this late again.

"Finally." I opened the door and walked into the living room.

"I got busy with some shit, what's up? What do we need to talk about? You handle the abortion, right?" He asked, standing near the door.

"Yes, I handled it. I took an Uber home, so I didn't need you to bring me."

"Oh." He nodded his head.

"Why are you just standing over there, Boss? Come sit down. I cooked."

"It smells good shorty, but I really have a lot of shit going on. I only made time to stop by to."

"To make sure I killed our fetus right." I cut him off and he dropped his head.

"You saying it like that makes it sound worse than what it is, Serenity. I came over here because you said you needed to talk. I can fuck with you another day, but I don't have time to chill over here tonight. I'm sorry."

"Fine." I turned my back to him.

"And I do have something to tell you if you would stop being so impatient and just listen." He walked up behind me and grabbed the back of my arm.

"Then turn your ass around and talk to me, Serenity. What's going on? I'm here, you act like I didn't show up."

I was going back and forth all day on whether I should involve myself in anything Boss and Francis had going on. But he was my boo, shit my soon-to-be husband if the lord says the same.

"Francis called me in her office today and said she's been having you followed. She asked me if I was fucking with you, and she said she is ready to take you down."

"She been having somebody follow me? Why the fuck you didn't tell me that before I came over here?" He scrunch up his face, pissed off with me.

"Baby I didn't want to tell you over the phone because how do we know that she's not tapping you on there too?"

He rubbed the top of his head.

"And what else did she say?"

"She wants to get you locked up for someone's murder. I don't know why she told me all of this when I'm loyal to you."

"I hope you are." He looked at me with curiosity in his eyes.

"I am loyal baby, that's a promise. We may be new but I'm not turning on you for anybody. Fuck that job.

"You right and fuck that bitch."

He pushed the barstool out of frustration. Boss finally went and sat down on the couch nearby and leaned forward staring at the floor. I walked up behind him and rubbed on the back of his head because I could tell he was stressing.

"It's going to be okay baby; she won't get nothing on you that will stick. She's just mad that she can't control you anymore."

"She's mad about a lot more than that, believe me, and I can't have that bitch out to get me for the rest of her miserable ass life. I need that hoe gone. She won't stop until I'm back behind bars."

"That's not happening."

"No, it won't. Especially if you help me take care of her. Get her before she gets me."

He replied, looking up in my face.

"Help you like how baby? What kind of plans were you thinking about?"

I continued rubbing on his back until he said, "Kill her." And I stopped rubbing in an instant.

"What do you mean kill her? You want me to go in and shoot the lady?" I asked in a panic.

"Nah, not anything like that. That's too obvious, we need her to get taken out in a way that won't ever be found out. I can hit up my boy Steez to find this white nigga who has some shit to kill her but on the low. I would need your help though. You got me?"

He asked, looking into my eyes as he grabbed my chin.

"Of course, I got you, baby, forever," I replied and he kissed me while holding the side of my face. Boss and I had only kissed while fucking, but we hadn't ever shared a kiss quite like this one before. I loved it and I felt like we were truly getting somewhere now in our relationship. I just don't know about this killing Francis thing, but I would make him think I would if that would make him fuck with me harder.

"Now, can you stay and try my stew please?"

"Yeah, I guess I could eat." He started taking off his jacket. I smiled hard ass hell going into the kitchen after he smacked my ass.

Time to fill his stomach so that I could eat his dick up and do anything else he wanted me to do for tonight.

Chapter 11

Kit

I was knocked out asleep in this chair when I felt someone tapping on my shoulder.

"Get your ass up, you're coming with me." He replied as he untied my wrist.

"Coming with you where? I thought y'all wasn't going to kill me if I cooperated?" I panicked, as my breathing started to labor.

"No, I'm not going to kill you. If I were going to kill you I would do it right here." He finally took off the zip ties on my ankles attached to the chair and stood me up. Steez then walked me to the side door they'd been coming in and out of and took me to his car.

"Am I getting in the trunk?"

He turned his nose up at me and jerked his neck back.

"You think I'm going to fall for that shit again? You getting in the backseat." He opened the door.

"Now lay down and if you try anything you will die. I don't give a fuck what Boss say." He replied, and for some reason, I believed him. The hierarchy of their gang was clear as day and Boss was running things. Then there's Steez, Mystic, and everybody else under them including that fuck ass nigga Ahmad I tried to deal with.

Growing up, I wanted to be like these nigga's simply because my brother Tony idolized them. When they gave him a chance, he took it too fast and ended up being an enemy on a debt he should've never had. That's one thing he and I never did alike. I wasn't careless at all with money. Had I not taken that shit about the shop to the cops then they still wouldn't have any idea about that. I was smarter than Tony. Smarter than all these niggas around the Chi.

Steez laid me down in the backseat and tied a zip tie around my ankles and hands. He cranked up his car and then started blasting that lame-ass Eminem music that I was tired of. We drove around for a good minute until the car came to a stop and Steez turned down the music.

"I'll be right here so don't think of trying shit." He said over his shoulder.

I laid there and closed my eyes noticing that wherever we were was quiet as hell and the only thing I could hear was sirens ringing in the distance.

"What's up, bro." I finally heard another nigga's voice.

After the sound of them slapping hands, I started to listen to see if these niggas were mentioning anything about killing me.

"So, Steez where you coming from my nigga? It took you all day to get here."

"Man, I have been busy babysitting this bitch for Boss. He running around fucking hoes and I'm stuck in this warehouse with his opp all day." I heard a lighter flick.

"Damn man. See, that's why we gotta get on our own shit how we were before he got out. I just got used to running shit then this nigga come home. We need to find our own plug and do our own thing."

"Shit, even if we do Boss has the streets sewn up. That nigga is going to have to have no plug at all to be taken out of the game."

"Well shit, let's do that then. Kill his plug and leave him out to dry." The other voice spoke as my eyes enlarged in my head. Was I hearing this correct? Was Boss's main nigga talking about snaking him with someone else?

"I don't know about all that bruh, but we will talk about it another day. You got that cash you supposed to be bringing me?"

"Oh, yeah. Here are the twenty bands. Appreciate that little murder you did for me last week. Now I get custody of my kids and everything else good."

"That's what's up."

I heard them slap hands again.

"Well let me get this bitch back to the spot before she tries to slip away again. I'll holla at you later though, we going to figure something out."

"That's a bet bro, one." Steez got back in the car and pulled off. I laughed to myself thinking about the peace Boss doesn't ever see. Being a kingpin in Chicago wouldn't ever not come with drama. I was happy to be out of the game, to be honest. You really can't trust anyone.

Riding in the back of this car wasn't that bad with the heater blowing and me not sitting up in that hard-ass chair. Steez was blowing a blunt in the air and the secondhand smoke was low-key relaxing me. My life right now was so pathetic that the bar on making me comfortable was low.

Steez was driving fast and hitting corners like a fool, so I was constantly rolling around the backseat. When Lose Yourself by Eminem started playing this nigga started driving even faster.

He had to be hitting seventy down the street until red and blue lights started flashing and Steez started to curse.

"Fuck, shit! Fuck!" Steez let out several curse words back-to-back. Steez pulled the car over and then leaned his head back against the seat. From down here, it looked like this nigga was praying.

Once the police officer came up to the window, he shined his lights in the front seat and then shined them in the back putting the bright light in my eyes.

"Show me your hands right now!" He yelled at Steez who raised his hands in the air. The police officer kept the gun on him as he opened the door still flashing the light in our face. Steez seemed to be complying with the officer until he suddenly pushed him against the door, grabbed his gun, and fired multiple bullets into his body. Steez quickly shut the door and then took off from the scene with his tires screeching loud as hell against the pavement.

"Fuck!" Steez was more in a panic as he hit the corners like a maniac. When I heard his phone calling out on speaker, I had a feeling he was calling the very man he just said he was tired of babysitting for.

"What up?" Boss answered.

"Yo, where you at boy? I just had to smoke a cop."

"A cop? For what nigga? I thought you were at the warehouse with that bitch. They came out there?"

"Naw, I brought her out somewhere with me. That's why I had to smoke him. Now I'm about to have to ditch the car and smoke this bitch so she won't say shit."

"Nah bruh, don't smoke her. I need her. I'll meet you somewhere to get y'all, where you at?"

"I'm hitting the corner on 55th and King now!"

"Alright, go to the flea market on Lincoln and Silver and wait for me behind that bitch. I'll be there in twenty minutes."

"Alright, bet!" Steez spoke before the phone disconnected. He kept cursing, hitting corners, and driving recklessly until we came to a complete stop. He turned the car off and started looking around.

"Man come on Boss, where the fuck you at nigga?" He talked to himself, unable to keep still. The more time went by the more impatient he started to get, and he took out a pistol and cocked it in the front seat.

Once again, I felt I was going to die.

"God please forgive me for all my sins. God, please forgive me for all my sins." I repeated back-to-back until his face lit up with car lights. He opened the back door, and they pulled me out of the backseat throwing me into the other car like a piece of luggage.

As I laid in the backseat, I heard them scrambling outside the car before I could see a large flame shoot up in the air. Boss and Steez then got in the car, and we took off away from the crime scene passing up a few sirens on our way.

I see now that these niggas moved like ninjas when the time comes, and I couldn't fuck with it. Whatever they wanted me to do I knew I had to, or I would be laying on the pavement just like that cop Steez just killed. That's if their operation lasts too much longer with snakes slithering around their camp.

I still however wasn't fucking with it. They got my loyalty for sho.

Chapter 12

Boss

After nights like last night, I liked to lay low and stay in the house out of the way. I didn't kill the cop but aiding in abetting with a cop's murder would get me just as much time.

I laid in the bedroom my mama set up for me after I got out. I thought about all the nights I spent staring at a wall just as I am now except walking out wasn't an option. When the memories of prison became too vivid, I sat up on the side of the bed and put on my house shoes. The freedom of being able to walk out of my room door still felt surreal. That and smelling bacon and sausage as soon as I hit the corner which I did because of my perfect ass mama.

"Good morning mama." I kissed her on the cheek.

"Good morning my only baby. Breakfast is almost ready. Just give me a chance to cook your pancake." She replied, grabbing a bowl and stirring in it. As the sounds of her food cooking and the low gospel music played, I grabbed my coat and stepped outside to make a call to Steez to make sure he was straight after last night. When I dialed his number, I stared into the space randomly spotting a camera out of the window down the street. Maybe it was for google maps or some other type of gentrifying ass shit Chicago had going on.

"Yo?" Steez finally answered the phone.

"You good, nigga?"

"Yeah."

"Well let me call you right back. Something just came up."

"Bet." He responded as I stepped down the steps to take a closer look at the cameraman down the street. When I got to the sidewalk, his car backed up and he did a U-turn in the street going the opposite way. This nigga was moving like the feds and more specifically an undercover fed. That or a private investigator.

I hadn't forgotten about what Lump said about Francis stalking me and now I'm sure I see it happening in front of my face. I couldn't kill a private investigator, but I could kill the bitch that's paying him. It was now or never with this hoe because I didn't like the idea of being followed.

I went back into the house and passed up the kitchen full of hot food because I now had something a little more important to handle than eating right now.

I put on some clothes and shoes and dialed the white boy's number who Steez had the hook up with. Harlow would be just the nigga I needed to see to give me what I needed to stop this bitch Francis from following me quick, fast, and in a hurry.

Harlow first helped us when Steez wanted to take out his stepdad to help his mama get the life insurance money. This shit he cooked up in his lab was untraceable in any autopsy and was masked as a heart attack or some other kind of cardiac issue. With Francis being a warden at the prison I knew I couldn't shoot the bitch down because it would cause too much attention. The cops would be looking into all prisoners recently released and especially the ones she had problems with. After all the disciplinary reports that bitch gave me, I would for sho be at the top of any list. If I could afford this poison for every murder I would, but bullets were way cheaper than an untraceable death. I only pulled out the big guns like this for people like Francis. Murders in the streets didn't get investigated so hard.

After I met up with Harlow and paid him twenty bands for this tiny tube of liquid poison I drove straight to Lump's house. She told me she had to go to work at 3:30 so that meant I had about an hour to convince her to help me murder this bitch today.

"After knocking on the door, I announced my name and she answered it, in her uniform pants and no top. I hugged her at the door and tongued her down as if she were Megan.

"Mm, hey baby." She smiled after I let go of her lips.

"I didn't know you were coming through right now, Daddy. I told you I have to work today boo."

"Yeah, I know you do, but I wanted to see you before. Plus, I have something I need to give to you." I placed the tube in her hand.

"What's this." It's that stuff you're supposed to give Francis remember?"

"The stuff to kill her." Her eyes became enlarged, and she sat on the side of the couch. I stood in front of her and grabbed her chin raising it so she could look up at me. Shawty started breathing heavily and I could tell she was panicking already.

"Never mind Lump, you don't seem like you ready for no shit like this."

"Of course, I'm not Boss. You're asking me to commit a murder."

"You're not committing murder. I am, and the nigga who made this shit. You just giving it to her. You said yourself she out to get me. Three drops of this shit right here and that bitch is gone. Don't you realize what she's trying to do by following me? Sooner or later her dumb ass is going to find something, and I will be locked up and in jail before you and I can try and build anything together."

"And I know that Boss. I'm just really scared is all. I don't want to go to prison, it's bad enough working there."

"Look I know it is and that's why if we ever get married, you won't be working there anymore." She lifted both her eyebrows as she looked at me with a hopeful expression.

"For real Boss, you mean that."

"Yeah, I mean it. No wife of mine is working in a place like that. That shit is for the birds and people like Francis who will keep niggas like me in there." I sat down on the couch beside her. I guided her into my lap with her arm, and she placed her head on my shoulder.

"Baby if I do this do you promise I'll be okay?"

"I wouldn't tell you to do anything like this if I didn't think so. That bitch out to get me and she told you herself. If I'm in jail, how am I going to eat that pussy the way you like it?" I kissed her on the neck. Her lips quivered from my touch, and I could tell right away she needed to feel me just as much as I needed her to do this shit to Francis.

"Take these off." I tugged at the waistline of her jeans. She stood up and slipped them off and I pulled my dick out of my pants stroking it as I looked up at her.

She attempted to sit down on my dick, but I stopped her.

"Nah, sit on my face. Climb up here." I leaned back against the couch as she climbed onto my face.

As soon as her lips touched mine, I started tonguing that pussy down and circling her clit with my tongue. I grabbed her big ass cheeks and pulled her closer to my mouth so that I could eat this mutha fucka better than she ever had it before.

"I'm cumming Boss! I'm cumming!" She yelled as she dripped her juices into my mouth and rose from my face. I got up after her and made her bend her ass over the couch so that I could fuck her pussy from the back. I started off slow at first and made her bring that ass back to me until she was used to it and ready for it all. Within a few strokes, my dick disappeared into her guts and the only noise that could be heard in the room was clapping. I grabbed her ponytail for a tight grip and stroked her until she sounded like she was losing her breath.

"Fuck Boss, you make me want to do anything for you Daddy!"

"That's what I want to hear but first, cum on my dick." I started fucking her faster and harder.

"Okay, baby! I will Daddy, I will!" She yelled, bringing me to a point where I was about to bust.

Lump came so hard on my dick it looked like a freshly glazed donut when I pulled it out. She laid there panting for a minute and then she turned around and sat on the couch watching as I rubbed my nut out onto her leg. After I was done, she stood up and got face-to-face with me.

"Tell me what I need to do, and I'll do it. But you have to promise me one thing."

"What's that?"

"You won't make me regret it."

"You won't, and if you do. It won't be because of me shawty." I kissed her on her lips. Lying to her was easy because I didn't have any true feelings for her. Besides liking to fuck the bitch, it went no further than that. She and I would be locked in for life but not in the way she wanted.

Chapter 13

Lump

The next morning.

When I walked through the prison doors I went through check-in and made it inside with the small tube of poison I needed to give to Francis. My hands were shaking, my knees felt weak, and I was trying my hardest not to punk out. My man needed me to do this, and I know for a fact he would love me forever for committing such an act.

I was nervous as hell walking down the long hallway to stand with my coworkers at turn out. Turnout was where everyone met before any shift to find out where we would be posted for the day. Where I was placed today was important because of what I had to do to Francis.

"Good morning, everyone, let's get right to it." Our Sergeant spoke up once everyone from our shift was there. He started assigning us our post and I prayed to God I was put in a position to do this today while I had my nerves built up for it.

"Lumpkins, you're in the cafeteria for chow until 8:00 pm and after that, you will join Ledecky in the towers until the end of your shift."

I nodded my head okay satisfied with my placement. Once they were done laying out rules, we were sent to our assigned areas, and I started patrolling the café as I usually do.

"Lump, did you have a bad morning or sum?" One of the inmates Green, asked as I passed by his table.

"No, I didn't. Why did you ask that?"

"I don't know. It just looks like you are."

"Looks can be deceiving. Now eat your food so you can go back to your cell."

I attempted to behave normally as I walked away from his table. When I saw Officer Blanchard walk into the kitchen, I knew he was putting in Francis's dinner request because it was 4:00. I walked in just in time to bump into him on his way out.

"You on your way back to the front until her food is done?" I made conversation to stop him. Being with coworkers for twelve hours a day, we all had pretty decent working relationships with each other.

"Hell nah. I'm not walking back that way until they give me her food tray. I'm tired. I have been on my feet all day. Her ass makes me sick sending me back here for this nasty ass food."

"Try telling her it's nasty. She thinks her meal plans and dietary system is the best in the state. She's crediting good health and weight loss inside the prison population to herself when it was really because of powder and meth being snuck up in here."

"No shit." Blanchard laughed with me.

"But you can go back up there now. I'll bring her tray up when I take Inmate Johnson to get his insulin. It should be in the next thirty minutes and her food should be done then."

"Okay, I appreciate you. Let me take my fat ass back to the front so I can leave this bitch on time tonight."

"I hear that. Have a good night, Blanch." I laughed with him as he walked away.

While her food was being prepared, I kept moving about the cafeteria as normal. I was having conversations with the other guards and yelling at the inmates every five seconds.

When I walked inside the kitchen, the main chef Patty smiled big with the last six teeth he had left.

"I'm here for Francis's food tray. Is it done yet?"

"Yes, finishing it up now." He scooped some green beans onto the tray.

"Tell Warden Francis she is going to love the way I seared that Chicken for her today. I used lots of butter and rosemary for a hell of a flavor." I laughed because this nigga really thought he was a chef.

"Cool, is it just this right here?" I pointed at her tray.

"Wait, let me get one more thing. Her piece of bread is still heating up in the oven." He walked around the corner, and I knew this was my chance to make a move if any. I took the tube from my hair and popped the lid off, sprinkling the solution all over her grilled chicken." After that, I put the tube back in my head until I could dispose of it in the restroom later.

Patty walked back from the oven with two pieces of toast on his spatula.

"Here we are. Thank you, Ms. Lump."

No thank you, I walked out of the kitchen with her tray on a cart. I then grabbed Johnson from his table to come with me to the front. We walked what was known as the long mile up to the infirmary and I sent him to get his insulin while I took Francis her food.

After buzzing the intercom, I nervously stepped back.

"Who is it?"

"It's Lumpkins, I have your meal tray," I replied, and she buzzed me in.

"Thank you, thank you, ma'am." She put the pen down on her desk.

"No problem. Patty told me to tell you that he cooked this with butter and rosemary today. He's super proud of this meal."

"Sounds good. I'm ready to enjoy it. I hope this new chicken vendor we switched to has better chicken than that last company." She looked at me over her glasses.

"Glad to see you're still coming into work. Usually, women who get caught up with hood millionaires, don't feel the need to work anymore."

"Oh, well, I absolutely do need to work. I'm single and I have real bills."

"Well, I hope you stay single if you have to choose men who just got out of here. You deserve way better than that."

"Thanks, I'll see you around," I replied, walking out of her office knowing I would never actually see her around again. That chicken, butter, and poison was about to block every chance of that happening. If she wasn't so nosey and invasive she would still be alive after today.

The next morning

When the sunlight shined through my bedroom window, I knew I'd slept in way too late. Work last night went by slow as hell with the entire prison on lockdown because Francis croaked at 10:11 pm. No one was around when she died, and Sergeant Mayer's is who found her sprawled out on her desk. After word spread around that she died I went into the bathroom and dropped to my knees to say a prayer. I cried silently shaking from head to toe scared of what was to come.

After my panic attack, I made my remorse take a backseat to my potential happiness in the future. I wanted to never think about that day and for it to never be brought up again.

Last night when I got off from work, I called Boss to tell him the news of Francis's passing, but he said he'd already heard it from someone inside the prison. I'm pretty sure it was Hollywood who'd told him before I got a chance too. Those niggas always had phones on the inside. Some of them I simply let get away with shit because I never wanted to deal with them on the outside.

It was my day off and after I cleaned up my entire house, I wanted to spend the day with my boo. As a matter of fact, I needed to call him now to see if he wanted to make plans with me outside of here. The movies or something would be nice.

"Hello." He answered.

"Hey baby, what are you up to?"

"I'm actually busy right now. Can I call you back a little later?"

"Yes, of course you can. I was just seeing if you wanted to go out and have dinner or a drink or something. I'm off today." I smiled, as I sat up on the side of the bed.

"Going out to have drinks after what we conspired isn't' the safest thing right now. Let's lay low for a lil' bit longer. We don't want to alarm people."

"You're right baby." I had to agree with Kim.

"Alright, well I'll get back at you later Shawty."

"Okay." We hung up the phone after speaking to each other. I got out of bed and slipped on my house shoes before going into the living room to start straightening up my house.

"Nigga what the fuck! You scared me!" I screamed seeing Darryl sitting in my living room.

"How the fuck did you get in here?"

"I know you never keep that window locked." He pointed to my window near the fire escape.

"Darryl, you need to get up and get ghost because I don't want you here! Why the fuck do you keep coming over here!"

"You can't tell me what to do. I'm starting to get real pissed off with your little attitude as if you're better than me. You think because you fucked with that fuckin criminal that you the shit. Serenity you ain't something a man can't find over and over again and I hope you know that."

"Darryl if that's the case then why are you here? Why are you acting like you can't just get up and go!"

"Because I don't want to!"

"But I do, so go!"

"Naw! Make me bitch!"

I slapped him in his face. He sat shaking his head while smiling until he suddenly went into a rage, and attacked me, knocking my body against the wall. He and I wrestled until we fell over my end table where my large stone-plated vase sat. While he manhandled me, I grabbed the vase and swung it at his head so hard it cracked up the whole side and he fell to the floor.

"I'm sick of your shit! You're not about to keep controlling me!" I yelled as his eyes went into the back of his head, and he passed out. I sat the pieces of the vase I still had on the table and stood over him. It was a bit confusing because I was breathing hard as hell after the tussle, but he didn't seem to be breathing at all. I shoved his body over with my foot and he didn't move an inch. I hope I didn't kill this man. And if I did, I was going to jail, unless I called the cops over here now. I picked up my phone and just as I was about to dial 911, Boss popped up in my head. I needed to call him because I'm sure he would know exactly what to do.

I dialed his number and when he answered I started crying.

"What's going on Lump?"

"Baby this crazy ass nigga has come over here again. I woke up to him in my house this morning."

"Call the police on that nigga. He's in your shit. Maybe this will help you get the police on your side. Use that damsel in distress shit to your advantage." Yeah, you're right." I looked at him still passed out on the ground.

"I have to go though; I'll call you later."

"Uh, okay but."

I couldn't get out anything else because Boss hung up the phone and I immediately started to feel a way. At least he did give me a piece of advice before he so rudely got off the phone.

Taking his advice, I dialed 911 and let it ring as I watched his body start to twitch on the floor. This mutha fucka wasn't dead so I'm for sure filing charges on his ass. This was the last resort before I had Boss kill him.

When the operator answered I was sure to cry a little bit to set the scene.

"I need help now. My estranged husband just broke in and attacked me."

"Okay, ma'am, calm down and give me your address."

"I'm in the Oak Towers, ma'am. Please send help."

"Okay, police will be there in a minute. Just stay on the phone with me until they arrive." She spoke calmly over the phone, and I waited near the kitchen next to my entire knife set.

When the cops got here, I let them inside, and they instantly called for an ambulance to help me and unfortunately his dumb ass.

They asked if I wanted to ride in the ambulance and I figured I had to say yes. After all, Darryl left here on a stretcher from whatever kind of concussion or coma I gave him with that lamp. He can't out victim me.

When I arrived at the hospital, I was taken to a room and given a gown so I could be examined from head to toe. A black female doctor came in which made me feel very comfortable as she began probing over my body.

"Does this hurt right here?"

I winced in pain when she pressed her fingers into my side. The idiot had punched me there, so it made sense as to why it was painful to the touch.

"Yes."

"What is the pain on a scale from one to ten."

"A nine, ten to be honest," I replied, as she nodded her head.

"Okay, so here's what we will do for you. We will perform an X-ray to see if you have any broken bones inside your ribcage. Then we will be able to assess all of the other pain you have. Your ribs are a very important injury that we want to check out as soon as possible. After all the ribs are guarding our lungs so a broken one can cause even more serious problems." I nodded my head as she laid everything out for me.

"So, I'll order your labs but one quick question. Are you expecting at the moment?"

"I was. I mean I thought I was and then he attacked me, and I bled, so I'm sure I miscarried. So no, the answer is no." I replied, and she pressed her lips together.

"Okay, so we would want to know for sure before we perform the X-ray. I'll have a nurse come in for a urine sample just to be sure beforehand. Just as a precaution." She replied, and I told her okay before she left out of the room.

I sat on the table biting my lip anticipating for this to all be over with. In no time a nurse came back in with a urine cup, and I went into the restroom filling the cup to the red line. The nurse took the sample and then came back to bandage up my arm as well as the gash on my knee. They tried to make me as comfortable as possible while we awaited the pregnancy test results. I laid there for about an hour and a half before the doctor came back into the room.

"I'm sorry for the long wait Mrs. Lumpkins. The lab in the hospital is usually slower at night. But I do have your results back and you are still in fact pregnant."

"Huh?" I was caught off guard.

"But I, I don't understand. I bled when he assaulted me."

"Yes, ma'am I understand that, but bleeding doesn't always indicate direct trauma to the fetus or your ovaries. You're pregnant and at least a month and a half so we will have to go about your rib testing in another manner." She went on but I tuned her completely out. When she left out of the room, I grabbed my phone to call Boss, and I saw that he'd texted me about an hour ago and I just didn't hear it.

Lump, I'm feeling you, but we for real need to chill for a minute with what we did today. I still fuck with you, and I appreciate you so never question that. I just want us to both stay free number one and number two know that what's meant for us is meant for us. I'll hit you back in the future when it's safe too. Remember everything stays between us and our relationship can still pick up in the future.

I read his message over and over again feeling dumber each time. Of course, this nigga was doing this right now after convincing me to abort the baby and commit fucking murder.

I can't take back what I did to Francis, but I bet he doesn't get a chance to convince me to kill my baby again. This dog-ass nigga won't know about the baby until it gets here. Then he won't have any choice but to care about us. It would hurt now but I will get everything I deserve later.

Chapter 14

Megan

When I walked out of those locked doors and saw Boss's car outside, I was happy, to say the least. The judge had given me a $50,000 bond and Boss had no issue paying $5,000 to get me out. When he saw me coming up to the car, he hopped out and hugged me as tight as I needed him to. All of our beef and troubles were put behind us right now because I needed all the support I could get.

We got inside his car, and I laid my head back against the seat feeling the cool air sail past my body.

"You hungry? Can I stop you somewhere?"

"Mm, not really. I'll probably be hungry a little later. Right now, I need a damn blunt."

"Here, take this." Boss lifted a freshly rolled joint from his center console. This was probably the first time I craved smoking weed in my life. My nerves were so shattered I could probably smoke some crack right now if it was around, shit I see how people could get on that shit. Being in jail for two days was the worst two days I've spent in my life. I don't know how I could possibly do any more time than that. Getting years would destroy me, mentally and emotionally. I just can't do it and thinking about it made my entire body numb.

"You feeling a little better now?" Boss asked as I exhaled my second puff.

"Yeah, I guess so. Thank you for coming through for me. I really appreciate it."

"Oh, you know I got you if I don't have anybody else. I have been waiting to hear your bond amount all day."

"Yeah, but now to the hard part. Do you know I was talking to a girl in there who is saying I could get up to ten years in prison for my charge? Boss I just can't." I got quiet before I started crying. The weed didn't do anything but make me high and emotional, but it hadn't made any fears go away. Boss reached across the seat and rubbed my thigh trying to comfort me as he drove.

"You going to be alright baby, don't worry about that shit. I promise I'm getting you out of this. I've worked on some things to get you out of this situation.

"Like what Boss?"

"Look, don't worry about it, Fox. I told you I got you and I meant that baby. Now sit back and enjoy your joint and today we are focusing on putting your mind at peace. Did you want to stop by to see your mama? I'm sure she's wondering why she hasn't heard from you in days unless you already called her."

"Nah, I didn't. I'm not fucking with her right now."

"Your mama, why?" Boss scrunched up his face. This nigga loved and adored his mama so much that I'm sure he didn't understand how anyone could be at odds with their mother.

"She has my dad staying there with her and she knows how I feel about him."

"Oh yeah, that's tough. Is he still on that shit?"

"No, he doesn't appear to be."

"Oh, well maybe that's why she's getting to know him again. Everyone makes mistakes but some folks change. You don't think he's changed?"

"Nope, someone like him never will, and she knows that." I crossed my arms because I didn't really want to talk about this either.

"Well, whatever he did I'm sure isn't enough to keep you from your mama. Go see your mama and don't fuck with that nigga, simple."

"Boss, you really don't know how unsimple this shit is. Even seeing him again would set me off. I hate I saw his ass the other day."

"Damn, sorry you feel that way, but again, I could never not speak to my mama, no matter who's around her. You better let that shit go and ignore that nigga."

"Boss you really need to shut up because you don't know what you're talking about."

"Naw, your ass tripping, and I'm standing on that. She's your mama and we only get one"

He finally made me snap.

"Yes, we only get one mother but she's laying up with a man who she knows sexually abused me when I was too young to even know what was happening to me! She knows that and he's still there so what does that tell you!" I yelled and he didn't say anything back this time.

"So yeah, we only get one mother but the one I got isn't as good as yours. I'm sorry." I replied, and Boss rubbed his hand across his head staring out of the windshield. I sat in my seat, breathing hard at this point from yelling at Boss with all the strength I had. I don't know how much time went by before Boss finally broke his silence.

"Fox, why haven't you ever told me about that?"

"Because I wanted it to go away just like he did. But now that he's back it's like a fresh wound is opened again. Then my mama."

I broke down crying so hard, Boss pulled over into the nearest parking lot.

"Boss my mama doesn't even believe me. She doesn't believe it happened to me and it did. I remember when he would do that shit. I used to hate being at home alone with him and she didn't care. How could you love a man that much?" I let out all my emotions as he rubbed my arm and kissed me on my forehead. His subtle whispers that everything was going to be okay were comforting at the moment, but I can't say I truly believed it would. After all, life has been crashing down on me since I found out about him and Yana, shit even back to when she first got shot in front of me. What was really going on in my life?

Once my tears stopped flowing so heavily, Boss and I went to the hotel we still had, and I jumped straight into the shower. I scrubbed my body from head to toe and then rinsed off with water almost too hot to the touch. I wanted to feel clean on the outside so maybe I could feel better on the inside. Plus, this showerhead was everything. This was the comfort I liked to live in. Not community showers in prison.

When I got out of the shower, Boss was sitting on the bed with his shirt off. Trying not to look at him sexually was hard especially since he had muscles now that he didn't have before he went in. He'd told me that he was working out a lot inside and seeing his perfect frame proved that.

"You feel a little better?"

He asked and I nodded my head.

"Good. You want me to hold you tonight?" He asked, holding his arms wide open in front of me.

"I don't know, I still don't know about us Boss."

"Megan, I know that I want you in my life and no one else. I want you to know that I'm here, that I care about you." He stood up and kissed me on the forehead. As much as I wished to fight it I couldn't. I laid my head on his chest and squeezed him so tightly that I'm sure it was hard for him to breathe.

"I'm going to go take a shower and I'll be out in a minute baby, so lay down and get comfortable." He told me and I did just that. I rubbed my feet together and drifted off while longing for Boss's warm body next to me. I still managed to go to sleep while he was in the shower and I'm not sure of how long I was knocked out before Boss was shaking my body to wake me up again.

"Aye, Meg. Megan."

"Huh?" I finally cracked my eyes open. This nigga probably wanted some cat.

"Hey, I just got a call, and I have to go up to the hospital where Yana is."

"What's wrong? Did she die?"

"No, she's not dead, she's off the ventilator and up talking. I have to take Adayah up there. She wants to see her."

"Oh," I replied, dropping my head. Why was I disappointed that she was alive?

"Okay, that's fine. You can go." I replied, sitting back against the headboard.

"Did you want to go? I know y'all are on rocky grounds right now but-."

"But nothing Boss, I'm fine. You can go. I know Adayah wants to see her mama." I waved him off trying to be the bigger person even though this hurt.

"Alright, I'll come back later tonight. I'm just taking her up there and I'll be back as soon as I can, alright?" I nodded my head okay even though everything was not okay. Tonight, was the night that I needed compassion and affection more than any other night and now he's having to leave just because of Yana.

This was a life I couldn't see myself adjusting to at any point in time. With my man, I wanted to be selfish and put on a pedestal no one could touch. Truth of the matter is now, I come second in Boss's life and because of that, I would never feel true happiness with him again.

Tonight, I am leaving this hotel and going completely underground to find the life I want to live. I'm not going to trial for my charge and I'm not sticking around for my life to get even worse than it is right now. If I have to live on the run from here on out, then I will. I just don't care about anything anymore.

Maybe I will find true peace and happiness somewhere that isn't Chicago.

Chapter 15

Kit

The next day

When Steez and Boss took me to the police station and let me out, they knew they had me right where they wanted me.

The plus side to getting that shit off Megan was that I would get immunity from any future gang violence from Boss or his crew. That meant I would have true freedom and living life without fear. Yes, I wanted to run inside this police station and tell them I was only retracting my statement because of their threats but I don't even think protective custody could keep Boss off of me. The only thing that could probably truly stop Boss is Boss, so being in his good graces was something I needed.

I walked up to the front desk and told the officers exactly what Boss told me too. They took me into an interrogation room and had me wait there for hours. I was sweating hard as hell, but I was ready to get this over with. When they came inside the room, I admitted to lying about it immediately and made them sit back in their seats looking defeated.

"So, you made everything up because you were a lover scorned? That's what you're telling me?" He asked after I gave him the entire run down.

"Yes, Megan didn't know about any of the transactions being recorded. I was over her books, and I did it to mask the drugs I was selling."

"This just doesn't make any sense to us. You come in here with phone conversations and tell us this elaborate story about your girlfriend's money laundering, and the records we found shows for that to be true. Now it's all a lie?"

"I didn't say it was all a lie, I'm saying I was doing it behind Megan's back. She is not into the life of crime. That girl can barely add let alone, tweak her books." I tried to downplay her intelligence.

The cops were looking at me like I was the craziest bitch they ever saw, and I couldn't blame them. Though some of this was true, me admitting to it was the dumb part.

I however had to man up at some point in my life. It would be a wild shot for the prosecution to still charge Megan since I am saying it was all on me.

"Alright, I'm going to talk to my partner to see where we go from here. Megan has already been bonded out, so she is not in police custody as of now." He pressed his lips together and walked out of the door.

When the cops came back into the room they stood over my chair and signaled with their hands for me to stand up.

"Kitina Harrington. You are being charged with Money Laundering and obstruction of justice. You have the right to remain silent, anything you say can and will be used against you in a court of law." He read me my rights.

I put my hands behind my back without a fight and felt okay with my fate. Where one day I wanted to get Boss back for all he's done to me and my family, I now realize Karma doesn't miss anyone. He will get his too one day and it will be much worse than we can imagine. Megan will also realize one day, who she should've chosen. Until then, I'll do my little time and come out of jail with my karma for killing Dezzy served. Then I will live a peaceful life happy and away from my troubles.

Chapter 16

Boss

One year later

Shorty cried as I shoved my dick inside her from the back. She was screaming as if I were killing her, but she was the one throwing her ass back like a maniac.

"Too much dick, too much dick."

I was seconds away from busting a nut and I sure as hell was pulling out even with a condom on. I didn't know this bitch like that. Shit, I just met her at the club three days ago.

After I nutted on her face, she licked around her lips and then smiled at me.

"Damn Daddy, you deserve everything good coming to your ass."

"Is that right?" I replied, taking off the condom and going into the restroom. I flushed my nut down the toilet because no hoe was catching me up ever again. Yana was the only baby mama I would ever have because I said fuck relationships since Megan disappeared on me a year ago.

"Come on shorty, let me walk you out."

I snapped my fingers as she laid across my bed.

"Really Boss." She groaned not moving fast enough.

"Yes, really. Now come on. I have to take a shower, and I don't know you to leave you out here alone, simple."

"Let me get in the shower with you then."

"But I'm still leaving right after that so you may as well go."

"Damn, so much for a round two later today huh?"

"Yeah, can't happen. I do apologize for the inconvenience." I replied as she got up rolling her eyes. I would maybe hit her up in the future or maybe I wouldn't. There were too many hoes in Chicago, so I wasn't just fucking on one if it's not the one I want.

After letting ol girl out, I locked the double doors on my condo and turned on my security system. Wasn't no one getting through that front door without me knowing it first and the windows were always safe since I was on the 13th floor. I decided to get somewhere of my own when bringing bitches back to my mama's house was no longer an option. I didn't go all out and get a penthouse, but my place was cool for me. Two bedrooms and two bathrooms with a patio overlooking the river.

Once I got out of the shower, I went into my closet and went through the racks to find something black to wear since I was leaving on demon time. Once I found a pair of pants and a black hoodie, I walked into the room and Alexa announced a call coming to my phone.

"Incoming call from, Steez."

She spoke and I went to the bathroom counter to grab my phone.

"What up?" I answered the phone.

"What up boss man."

"You out there?"

"Yeah, and I see that dirty mutha fucka now. He walking up the street with her mama. Both of them look strung out." Steez replied, telling me some of the exact words I needed to hear.

"Alright bruh, I'll be there as soon as I can."

"No problem, I'm eating a cold-ass pizza puff and listening to this podcast anyway so take your time." I laughed at what this nigga felt like was a good time. I wish like hell that I could just eat food, and chill by myself like Steez. That nigga didn't have any drama in his life which is how I wished to be.

After getting dressed, I got in my little throwaway car down the street from my condo building. Then I drove to the Southside where my target was. No matter how much time had gone by, I still wanted to get this nigga. With the shit he did it's forever up and stuck with his fuck ass. I went to sleep every night dreaming about this day.

Once I made it up to the hood, I pulled up to Steez who rolled down the window to talk.

"He's standing in front of that white house two doors down from their house in a red jacket. There's a bunch of kids playing down the street so be careful nigga.

"Oh, you know I am. No kids dying on my behalf. I appreciate you looking out though bro. I have something big planned for us in the next month."

"Bet."

"Alright, my nigga."

I replied, grabbing my AK from under the seat. I drove up a little closer to the yard of feigns standing around a fire by Megan's mama's house. There I had a perfect shot of her punk-ass daddy who didn't deserve to breathe any longer.

I let down the window and pointed my gun at him. I pulled the trigger and started ripping his red flannel jacket into shreds. His body jerked in the air as the other niggas ran off trying not to get taken out by gunfire. I fired so many bullets his way you would think I was trying to take out the entire block, but I have a little girl, and I can't understand how someone would hurt their child. Any nigga like this deserved to die and in the exact way.

Once he was full of holes I burned off from the scene. Nowadays I made sure niggas was dead unlike that bitch Kit. If she taught me anything it was to make sure my opps were dead before leaving the body. Though I was still pissed about that I can say that her being alive helped Megan in the best way. Megan avoided jail time, but the sad part is her ass is now avoiding me. Not for long though, her daddy dying will give her no choice but to come back to Chicago and I had a plan once she gets here.

After leaving their street, I drove all the way to the north side to ditch the car behind an abandoned corner store to torch it. Mystic met me over there to help and then we burned off from the crime scene as smoothly as we did the first time we got away with murder. This was simple work for us.

After I went home and cleaned myself up, I traveled straight to Yana's apartment to see my daughter. She'd been calling me since this morning asking for everything she could think of with her spoiled ass. So, on my way over there I stopped at the candy store by their complex to get her favorite lemonade gummy bears that she loved. After coping a bag of them I went straight to her house and up the steps to knock on her door.

"Who is it?"

"Boss," I yelled back to Yana who had to unlock all five locks to open the door. Ever since the shooting her once carefree ass was paranoid and shook as fuck. She was doing hair out of her house but only for certain customers. I told her that her ass would be alright if she didn't fuck woman's husbands, but she forgot that important part, so she always felt immediate doom.

When she opened the door, she smiled at me with the big ass cheeks her daughter inherited.

"Oh, hey, she's been asking about you all day." She held a comb, and some type of hair spray tucked under her arm. The entire apartment smelled like burnt-up hair and the lady in the chair looked like her ass was asleep.

"What y'all been up to?" I asked, walking behind Yana.

"I have been doing hair this evening and your child has been working my nerves. Did you hear about Duke, Megan's daddy getting killed earlier today?"

"No, I didn't. He really got smoked?"

"Yep, I would feel bad about it, but she didn't fuck with him anyway."

"Yeah, she didn't, so oh well." I shrugged my shoulders.

"Well anyway, what's in your hand daddy of the year?"

"I got her some of those gummy bears she likes from that candy shop around the corner."

"Ouu, I wish you would've gotten me some. You know your child doesn't share."

"Yeah, she got that only child syndrome bad."

"You ain't lying."

Yana replied, just as Adayah came running from the other room.

"What's up big girl."

"Hey Daddy" she crossed her little arms and stomped her foot.

"You took too long."

"I'm sorry baby, Daddy had to do a little work. I'm all yours now. Look what I got you"

I handed her the gummies before sitting down on the couch.

"Yummy, yummy, yummy." She danced and hummed to herself as she started stuffing gummy by gummy into her mouth. I was leaning back on the chair relaxing until I got a call from Steez who was always a must answer.

"Yo, what up?"

"Meet me at the trap nigga. It's important."

"Somebody hurt?"

"Yeah nigga, get here." He hung up the phone. I didn't move in a hurry for anybody but him. Steez was my right-hand nigga for many reasons, but his patience was number one. So, if he rushed, I knew it was for a reason. Especially when we just pulled a hit about two hours ago.

"I have to go mama, but I'll be back."

I kissed Adayah on her cheek.

"Bye baby daddy, be careful," Yana told me and I left their apartment building to drive back to the hood.

Once I got to the trap, Steez was standing outside against his car.

"We got a problem bruh. A big muh fuckin problem."

"What's wrong? What's going on?" I leaned back against the car with him.

"The nigga Garcia that we were getting our product from just got ran down in Cali. The word is, they took all his dope too. So, after a while, we won't have product anymore. At least not the good shit we've been giving out through the city. I wonder who killed this nigga bro."

"Damn, that's the only nigga we know who ship cane?"

"That's the only nigga we can trust. Even when you got locked up, he kept the operation one hunnit with me. The feigns going to know if the dope, is not the same and our rep is all we got."

Steez replied as I scratched my head trying to think of a quick solution to this major ass problem. Selling drugs was sticky because feigns and dope boys are mostly loyal to the good product. Because I was the one who always had the best, I became who I am in the streets today. There were very few plugs with flawless product and delivery methods like Garcia.

"I would suggest the man those boys out west Kilo and them used to deal with, but I heard that nigga only does pick up way in Memphis."

"Nah we ain't fucking with that." I thought a little more until I had an epiphany.

"You know, I wonder who Kit was dealing with because that product I stole from her sold out in a week."

"Who knows, shit it's only one way to find out. Ask the bitch herself, she is not dead.

Remember her ass tried to offer her plug up when that gun was up to her head anyway." Steez replied, taking a long hit from a black and mild. That nigga was stressing but I wasn't going to sweat about the shit.

I was going to do my research in the streets for a new plug and if I can't find one then I'm going straight to the women's prison where Kit was doing a five-year bid to get the hook up off her.

Chapter 17

Megan

The next week

Since my mama and daddy were never married, I was his next of kin. When my aunt Cathy called me and asked if would I come sign for his body to be released, I almost told her no. I hadn't been to Chicago and over a year and I was finally finding myself down in Nashville. I got on a plane a year ago and hadn't looked back to this city or the people here. The scent, the weather, and the memories were something I did not miss. I definitely wanted to be in and out of this place I left behind as quickly as possible.

Down in Nashville, I was doing white lady's hair which consisted of mostly bleaching and dying their roots to be beach blonde in a shop full of about six. I went into the shop every day. Build my clientele through a Facebook group from their city and made a decent amount of money per month. I was lonely and bored most of the time, but I couldn't find trouble there and trouble couldn't find me.

When I got off the plane, I took an Uber up to the Corner's office where his autopsy had been performed.

When I walked into the office, I grabbed my number from a ticket machine and sat down in the lobby until I was next up to the window.

"189." The lady finally called my number, and I walked up to the counter. Her face looked familiar, but I didn't know if I knew her or not. Often times I would see old clients that I couldn't put names to.

"Hello, how can I assist you?"

"Hey, I'm Megan Fox, I'm here to sign Dennis Fox's remains over to the Lincoln mortuary," I replied and she smirked which kind of threw me off. What was funny about this?

"Okay, just one second." She started clicking through her computer screen.

"Give me a little bit to pull all of your paperwork. You can have a seat until I call your number again."

"Okay."

I sat down, filing through my scheduled appointments to pass time.

I had to go back to Nashville in two days and I would be working as soon as I stepped off the plane. I would've left tomorrow had the flights not been ridiculous only because it was a Saturday.

My visit was going to be low-key and out of the way. I had a nice little hotel and plans to order DoorDash the entire weekend. I wasn't even going to Portillo's to get my favorite pizza. I couldn't risk being seen by anyone.

I watched as other people were helped quickly while I waited and waited for my number to be called. When I was one of the last people left in here, the lady finally called me to the front with a pamphlet of papers in her hands.

"May I start by seeing your I.D. please?" She asked, and I went into my purse and handed it to her.

"Okay, you will need to sign on all the Xs please."

"No problem, do you have a pen?" I asked and she slid it across the counter.

I signed my name on all the lines I was supposed to and then she signed in the spots marked for the office.

"Okay, thank you and we will get these filed for you and let you know when the death certificate is available. You may also tell the funeral home that they will hear from our office within twenty-four hours to schedule pick up."

"Okay, thank you."

I replied before I walked out of the door. When I got outside, I pulled out my phone to call an Uber when someone whistled in the near distance. Looking around, I was confused as to who it was until I saw Boss standing behind a Bentley looking my way.

"Do you want me to take you where you need to go?"

"Boss, how the fuck did you know I was up here?" I walked over to him with my face torn up.

"I knew what happened to that perverted ass nigga and I knew there was a chance you would have to come sign for his body. Being his only child and shit."

"That doesn't explain why you're here right now. Like at the same time as me." He rubbed his hand in his beard that had grown in thicker on his face. It didn't look bad though. It was clearly well-groomed.

"I paid ol girl that works in there to call me if you came into the office. When you got here earlier, she texted me that she would hold you here until I came." He flashed a big smile.

Boss had on clear glasses that were trimmed in silver and a platinum Cuban link to match. His beanie was tucked under all the way around and he had on an *off-white* brand coat that I'm sure was thousands of dollars. Today he had that shit on, but that still didn't take away from the fact that he was unhinged. With everything he did today to see me, he was starting to look like a true stalker for his efforts.

"Boss, I didn't come here to rekindle anything or to fall back into any old habits with you. The reason I left here was because I needed peace. Peace, you can't give me no matter how good you look or how bad you want me."

"It's past a want Megan, I need you in my life. Everything I've done over the past year I've done in hopes that I could have you back in my life one day."

"Why Boss? So, you can lie to me? Cheat on me, abandon me for the streets."

"Megan, lying and cheating would be out of the door if I get you back. All I ask for is another chance. I want to protect you and bring you that peace you say you want. Believe me, I can change for you." He pleaded as he placed his hand on his chest.

"You say that, but you can't keep your dick in your pants. I don't think you even have a mind of your own. I think your penis thinks for you."

"It used to be before I realized one good girl is worth more than a thousand bitches. I can admit, I've been with plenty of women since you disappeared but none of them would be worth breaking up our happy home. I would throw them bitches away so fast for you real shit, Megan."

"Boss, you just don't understand where I am mentally. I'm no longer the Megan you first met at that strip club years ago. Life isn't as materialistic to me as it was then, and I am happy being out of the limelight. I don't want to be seen by everybody anymore."

"Megan, I don't do anything but go home, let the money in the streets make itself, and take care of my kid. That's it, that's all. I'm not in the limelight either baby." He spoke on Adayah who I'd actually missed seeing.

"How is she?"

"Who, Adayah? She's good, she's growing up too damn fast if you ask me."

"I bet she is," I replied, and Boss grabbed my hand.

"Megan, listen. I can't ask you to forget about our past, so all I can do is ask you to give me a second chance at making you happy. Can you please believe in me? Let go of the past and understand I can change. I'll show you."

"Boss, I don't think you know what true happiness is. You know how to make women smile, you know how to make a woman feel good, and you sure as hell know how to make us feel beautiful, but there is more to making someone happy than those things. Good dick and conversation doesn't feed the soul."

"Well, teach me what does. I'm willing to learn."

"Okay, and what about Adayah? Did you forget about her?"

"I will never forget about her. All I ask is that you accept her as yours. Don't hate her because of what she came from."

"I would never hate her! You know that."

"Well, why can't you just move past the circumstances and be a family with me? I want to have a house with a wife and kids one day. This street life getting old." He replied, and I was shocked by his revelation. I never thought I would hear him say that.

"Even if I let the guard down around my heart, my mind will still think about the betrayal. Have you ever even got a test for her Boss?"

"Megan, she's mine."

"And how do you know that? Yana was fucking plenty of other people around that time. Trust me, I know."

"Megan, we did a test when I was inside. She purchased a kit which was administered by the nurse in the prison and sent to the labs."

"And who administered her part?"

"Megan, Adayah is mine, let's just stop this conversation." He stopped my questioning as if he was becoming irritated.

"Alright, but I should be going now. It's cold out here anyway." I started walking away.

"Let me take you where you going. I know you trying to cancel me out, but I haven't given up on us yet. I even have something in my pocket that I would love to give you to show you how serious I am. Give me one more shot Meg."

Boss looked at me with a soft sadness behind his beautiful eyes. I don't think I've ever seen him this vulnerable, but I also felt like I couldn't let his words affect the decision I made for myself a year ago. I couldn't choose him over myself anymore.

"Boss I'm sorry but I'm done with you, or the idea of us. If you love me, then you'll just let me go. No more stunts to see me, no more calls or texts. Just let me be happy without you. That's all I ask."

He dropped his head and shook it slowly.

"Okay, alright. I understand Megan. I guess I have no choice but to let you go."

I gave him a half-smirk and mouthed the words, thank you, because for some reason I couldn't speak.

I finally walked away from him and where I expected him to call my name he didn't.

Hopefully, this was the end of him pursuing me because I so desperately wanted to move on.

When the Uber arrived, I climbed inside putting my airport hotel as the drop-off destination. We were riding in silence when the radio started playing *Unthinkable* by *Alicia Keys* and I got emotional. I wanted so badly what the lyrics were saying.

"So, what brings you to Chicago?" The Uber driver interrupted my thoughts from the front seat.

"My dad got killed and I had to come to sign some paperwork."

"Oh, I'm sorry to hear that. My condolences to you and your family."

"Thank you so much, Darryl." I read his name off the Uber app.

When I looked into the rear-view mirror, I saw the kindest eyes looking back at me. He had a low haircut, a mustache, and brown sugar skin that looked as brown as coffee. He was handsome, but most of all he wasn't my type. That m was a plus these days.

"So Darryl, how long have you been driving Uber?" I read his name from the app.

"I would say about a year now. Ever since I got laid off from the prison. I like it, it's cool." He nodded his head to Maxwell playing in the background.

"That's good."

"And you are?"

"I'm Megan, does it not say my name on the app?"

"No, no, it does. It's just I pick up a lot of riders who aren't riding under their own account."

"Oh, yeah, that makes sense." I nodded in agreement.

"But anywho, it's nice to meet you, Ms. Megan."

"Nice to meet you too," I smirked in the mirror almost positive that I would be smitten by this man before my ride was over.

He had given me a good vibe from the jump.

Chapter 18

Yana

Today was one of my first days fixing myself up and looking like something in a very long time. Adayah was taking pictures at this studio that Boss set up and I wanted to be there to change her hairstyles in between sets. Boss picked us up because he knew me, and driving wasn't the best of friends now since my anxiety was always through the roof. I preferred to be a passenger princess now and especially to him.

When Boss told us to come outside, we walked down the steps, and he got out of the car to open the door for us which always warmed my heart. It felt especially good to see my baby loved by a man. I never actually had that growing up.

"What's been going on with y'all two?" Boss asked, after getting back into the car.

"Nothing much baby daddy. I see you got fly today, you taking pictures too?"

He laughed at me hyping him up. To be honest, Boss being fly was an everyday thing. I've never seen this man not look good. Any time he came over he made me feel self-conscious about my appearance. He knew what it was though, he's seen me at my best plenty of times.

As we drove to the location of the shoot, I kept looking over towards him as I always did anytime he was around. It used to be so hard not to do it when Megan was present because he had a magnifying presence. Though I never had these feelings for him before the threesome, they were powerful now. What was supposed to be a drunk nightcap turned me on to my strongest obsession. Wanting what I couldn't have was almost driving me insane at night.

"Mommy, can we get ice cream after this?"

"No, remember you wouldn't eat your spaghetti last night and I told you no sweets today."

"No, mommy! Please! I need ice cream." She whined from the backseat. My mama always told me she was exactly as I was when I was a little girl. I guess this is my karma for always being a brat my whole life. I couldn't help it though; I was the only child just as Adayah is.

"Don't worry about it, lil mama." Boss looked at her in the rear-view mirror.

"Daddy going to get you some food and ice cream immediately after the shoot if you take pretty pictures. Don't pay attention to your mean ass mama." He cut his eyes away from the road to look at me and I playfully punched him.

"You are not making her act any better, Boss. I'm going to send her with you full-time."

"Don't threaten me with something I want anyway." He shrugged his shoulders.

Seeing Boss be a father made him even finer than he already was to me. Around our baby, he was gentle, sweet, and less gangster than he was any other time. This past year since the shooting I've done nothing but fall in love even more with my ex-best friend's man.

Megan and I hadn't spoken since the day Debra shot me. I thought I would get to see her in court as a witness or something, but Debra took a plea deal and there was no trial. I won't lie and say I didn't miss my friend. I hated the way things turned out between us because she was my homie, the one person I could call about anything. That's why being in love with Boss was always so hard for me. I wanted to talk to her about him as I do everything else, but I couldn't. I instead had to pretend that I wanted them to be together. The whole time, I secretly wished it was me.

Now that she's gone, I miss her, but I didn't yearn for her presence. Her being gone allowed me to build a relationship with Boss without feeling bad about it. I was able to flirt with him without watching my words and stare deeply into his pretty ass eyes as he spoke. My life was finally starting to make sense, and I see it took her leaving for that to happen.

When we got to the studio, Boss jumped out of the car and opened the door for me first, then he went to the back to open the door for his princess. We walked inside and were greeted by the staff at the studio.

"Hi, mom and dad. Hi beautiful." The photographer Joy spoke to us.

"So, were going to go ahead and get her changed into the first outfit. I spoke with your husband about the process, but I'll go through it with you as well."

"He's not my husband but you can continue."

"I do apologize." She gave me an almost sympathetic reaction and continued telling me the motions. When she was finally done explaining and we went inside the changing room and Boss was quiet. Too quiet so I knew something was wrong. Most likely it was something to do with Megan.

Because she was once my friend, he often came to me to vent about her. They didn't have any interactions from what I know, but he still seems to be in love with her. She however gave him no time of day anymore.

"What's wrong? Why are you being so quiet?"

"Nothing is wrong, I was just thinking about something is all." He shook his head.

"Thinking about what?" I was slow to ask.

"Us. When that lady called me your husband it almost felt right. Us being a family and what not"

"You mean, you feel you're supposed to be my husband?"

"Yeah, I guess so." He made me start to get extremely nervous out of nowhere. Where was all of this coming from? Better yet where was it going?

"Boss I, I don't know what to say."

"Just say you will marry me so that we can actually give our daughter the home you and I missed out on growing up. Yana, I know we haven't been on no couple shit, but I don't mind trying if you don't."

"Really Boss?"

"Yeah, I mean we might as well. I have this ring for you. Been carrying it around for days. It belongs on your finger Yana." I placed my hand up to my mouth in utter shock as Boss pulled a ring box out of his pocket.

"Why does mommy get a present and not me?"

"Because I hope that we can all be a family if mommy takes this ring. I'm ready to show the world that I can be a family man for the women I love."

I shook my head as I held my hand over my mouth.

"Take it, mommy! Daddy bought it for you!" Adayah cheered happily not knowing my mind was made up the first time her father ever made love to me.

"Of course, I will. Of course, I'll marry you, Boss."

"Good, that's what I needed to hear, mama." Boss took the ring out of the box and slid it up my finger. He hadn't gotten down on one knee and there wasn't

a romantic scene with candles and flowers and such but my heart was still on cloud nine. I didn't expect this shit to happen ever and especially not today. I guess he was finally over chasing Megan after all this time.

"Aww, my little family, I love y'all." I hugged Adayah and went to sit on Boss's lap. I hadn't done this I don't think ever, and it felt so good to finally be here. It was sort of like mounting the throne I always knew was mine. I went in to kiss him on his lips and he kissed me back making Adayah start to laugh uncontrollably. She'd never seen us kiss before so I'm sure this caught her off guard.

"Thank you for making my day baby daddy." I rubbed my hand on the side of his face before kissing him again. I hated to be lying to this perfect man about Adayah being his child, but this shows it was all worth it in the end. The fake DNA results truly came in handy and now we get more than weekly visits with him at the prison.

We get to be a family, and I finally get to have that happiness with a man I always wanted to be mine.

Chapter 19

Boss

Two weeks later

When I woke up, I grabbed my phone from the floor nearby to see if I missed anything while I was knocked out last night. After rubbing my eyes, I saw I had a text from and unknown number along with text from Mys and other homies from the block. There was a photo attached to the message from the unknown number and I saw it was a baby boy with a sign that read four months beside him.

Who is this?

I wrote back and waited for the person to respond. At that time, I got out of bed and went into the restroom to piss as quietly as I could since Adayah was in the bed with me and Yana. She slept with us every night and I didn't complain because I hadn't built up the nerve to fuck Yana yet. I guess I was waiting to see how Megan would react to the engagement. Would she want me back after our engagement photos are posted? Only time will tell.

After pissing, I washed my hands and then brushed my teeth because I planned to get in the streets early. Being a family man now I didn't want to stay out too late. My little boss Adayah called me around 9:00 every night to come tuck her into bed.

After sneaking out of the room quietly I went into the kitchen to eat some cereal. I have to get Yana to wake up and have breakfast done early like my mama one day. Right now, I could use some eggs, grits, and orange juice this morning, but I guess Corn Pops would do.

After pouring my cereal and milk I sat at the dining room table and opened my phone up to catch First Take which was airing live right now. After pushing play on an episode and laughing at Stephen A for a while, another message popped up from the same number that sent that pic of that random baby earlier.

Boss, this is Serenity, well Lump as you used to call me. Is this you?

Before I could respond she sent another text that really through a nigga off. I hadn't saw or spoke to Lump in a year. She disappeared at the same time as Megan did and I wasn't too concerned about her. I figured she got spooked and fled Chicago after helping me with Francis. That's exactly what I wanted anyway.

Boss, if this is still you then I want you to meet, Javir Grayson, he's our son.

I read and sat back in my seat. I pushed the bowl of cereal away because my entire appetite was gone. That bitch told me she got rid of the baby she was pregnant with by me. Did this bitch think I was dumb?

Shawty find you something else to do. I haven't touched you in over a year.

I wrote back and I could see she immediately started to type.

Boss, he's four months old and trust I don't have to lie to you about who his father is. I tried to do this on my own, but I can't, and I need help. You and I at least need to meet up and talk about this. I see how good you take care of your other child. Javir deserves that too.

She responded, and I put my phone on the counter. It was too early for a conversation like this, and I was low-key wondering if I was dreaming. I had to be because there's no way this hoe Lump hid an entire pregnancy from me. Maybe I'll wake up after my shower.

Later that day

I never texted Lump back because I didn't feel like dealing with her at the moment. I had shit to do in the streets starting off with finding a new plug.

Nothing Lump said meant much to me because she was clearly trying to put a baby off on me and I would believe it when it's proven through court.

When I left the hood for the day, I drove back to my condo to get Yana and my baby so that they could get something to eat. I tried to get them to order delivery, but Yana said she wanted her food fresh. Her little ass was greedy as hell, and she passed that shit down to her daughter.

We drove down Clark Street until Yana finally spoke up

"I guess we will eat at McDonald's baby."

I nodded my head okay, and then put my signal on to turn into the restaurant. When I turned in, I noticed that the car behind us turned into McDonald's too. They didn't hop in the drive through line, they just parked in a space nearby.

"Welcome to McDonald's. Can I take your order?"

"Yes, give me a second. What do you want?" I looked at Yana.

"Now Boss you know you should just let me tell them since your patience is nonexistent." She laughed because I usually got frustrated ordering anything for her picky ass.

Yana leaned over me and stuck her head out of my window placing the most difficult order you can make at a fast-food spot.

"No onions, no ketchup, and please please no pickles."

She spoke to the cashier who was having a hard time hearing her. While she was talking to the microphone, I focused on the car that turned in behind us because no one still hadn't gotten out yet. Maybe I was being paranoid but I had a funny feeling about them.

"Anything else for you ma'am?"

"No thank you."

"Okay, pull around." The cashier spoke and Yana sat back in her seat. I pulled around the building and paid for the food still keeping my eyes on the car that was doing some funny shit.

When the workers handed us her food, she started grubbing and I reached over to grab a fry.

"Oh my God. Here, babe, you can have them. These fuckers have too much salt."

"I'm good, just needed to raise my blood pressure up like yours." She laughed at me. I was making small talk with her, but my eyes were in the rearview mirror the whole way out of the parking lot. The car however didn't move after me so I relaxed a little.

When I pulled up back in front of my condo, I got out of the car and walked around to the back to get Adayah out of the car.

"You can give her to me so that you can park the car?"

"You sure you can carry all that."

"Yes, babe." She replied before I handed Adayah to her. As soon as I walked back to the driver's seat, I heard tires screeching nearby and Yana's eyes grew twice their size on each side.

"Boss! Get down!" She yelled, diving to the ground before bullets started piercing my body back-to-back.

After the shooting stopped, Yana jumped up from the ground screaming while she bent down over me.

"Somebody help me! Help!"

I heard her screaming but I couldn't feel shit. I could see it was bad from the look in Yana's eyes and the fear in my daughters. Their faces were the last thing I saw before I closed my eyes. Their screams started to fade into the background and my entire life started to flash before my eyes.

To be continued

Claimed By The Hood Millionaire 3:

The Finale

To keep up with release dates join my READERS GROUP at the link below.

Black Lavish Readers Group

Made in the USA
Columbia, SC
02 February 2025